D1742515

# SOLITARY MAN

## THE SMITH BROTHERS #3

### SHERILEE GRAY

Copyright © 2020 by Sherilee Gray

All rights reserved.

Editor: Karen Grove

Proofreading: Judy's Proofreading

Cover Design by Cover Couture:

www.bookcovercouture.com

No part of this book may be reproduced in any form or by any electronic or mechanical means, including information storage and retrieval systems, without written permission from the author, except for the use of brief quotations in a book review.

This is a work of fiction. Names, characters, businesses, places, events, locales, and incidents are either the products of the author's imagination or used in a fictitious manner. Any resemblance to actual persons, living or dead, or actual events is purely coincidental.

Solitary Man - Sherilee Gray - 1st ed

# AUTHOR NOTE

Welcome back to the Smith family! If you're here with me now, it probably means you love big, dirty, growly, cinnamon roll heroes like me. YAY! I only ever intended for there to be two books in this series, but then Cash Smith popped into my head and once an idea takes hold...well, let's just say I can't be stopped. SO despite the series name, there are only two Smith Brothers lol. BUT there are quite a few cousins floating around. Which means, there could be more Smiths coming your way in the future! Just yanno, ignore the series name. Thank you for taking a chance on Solitary Man. I hope you love Cash and Riley as much as I do! x

# 1

## RILEY

TODAY, I was marrying a man I'd never laid eyes on before, not in the flesh, anyway.

No, I hadn't lost my mind, and no, this wasn't some creepy internet scam. We'd met through a reputable site. Also, and most importantly, I knew deep in my bones, in my soul, that this was exactly where I was meant to be. Today, I would meet and marry the man I would spend the rest of my life with.

I was coming home—metaphorically speaking.

Fate had led me to Cash Smith. It was no accident that I'd found him when I'd needed him most, and no one could tell me otherwise. Life was just a series of events, some wonderful...some not so wonderful.

I'd had more than my fair share of the not so wonderful parts. Cash was the good I'd been waiting a long time for— the good that I'd started to think would never come.

I clutched the emails he'd sent me over the last few months. I'd printed them out and had probably read them a hundred times. As a romance writer, I more than appreciated his way with words. My husband-to-be was open, intelligent, interesting, and I couldn't wait to meet him in person.

Tilting my head back, I let the sun warm my face and breathed in the clean Rocky Mountain air. I had an excellent imagination, but this place surpassed anything I'd dreamed up when I thought about a new life: landscapes that stole your breath, wide-open spaces, the sounds of nature moving at its own pace. The peace and quiet I'd been longing for. I'd have endless inspiration for my writing. But it was more than that. I'd have someone to share all this beauty with, someone who would be my partner in every sense of the word.

Cash and I had mainly communicated through email since he had such patchy internet out here, but I'd liked that. We'd gotten to know each other without any of the usual games that came with dating, without all the worry about outward appearances. Though, of course we'd exchanged pictures. And I had most definitely liked what I'd seen. My belly squirmed. He was tall with broad shoulders and rich chocolate brown hair. He also had the prettiest blue eyes I'd ever seen.

"Pretty" was an odd word to use for a man like Cash. But I couldn't think of any other word to describe them. When I saw those gorgeous blue eyes, they'd literally stolen my breath.

He'd also called a couple of times. His satellite phone had been fuzzy and crackly, but we had managed to talk a little—or more, I'd talked his ear off from nerves and excitement and barely let him get a word in—but I'd liked his voice. It was deep. Soothing.

I stood and stretched, then smiled down at the sweet gold and diamond ring he'd sent me.

"Cash shouldn't be much longer, honey," Landon, the

owner of the general store I was sitting outside, said from the door.

He'd introduced himself when I'd arrived, had told me Cash would be a little late and went back inside. He was holding two steaming mugs now, and he lifted one. "Hot chocolate?"

My smile widened, and I quickly tucked the emails back in my bag. I took the drink. "I love hot chocolate. I think I might be addicted to it."

He chuckled. "You might want to try it first. It could be terrible."

I took a sip and sighed. Heaven. "This is exactly how I like it. Exactly."

"Glad to hear it." He sat on the bench, and I sat back down beside him.

"So, you're getting hitched today, huh?"

"Yes." Nerves exploded through me, but they were the good kind.

My parents' voices echoed through my head.

*Oh, you're getting married? That's nice. Sorry, have to go. We have dinner reservations. You know how it is.*

*Click.*

That was it. They didn't even pretend to care anymore. Not that they ever did. They certainly wouldn't dream of tearing themselves away from their latest adventure to be there for me when I got married.

It still managed to hurt, though, despite all the years of neglect. Despite knowing better. I'd spent a lot of my life alone. Lonely. An only child with parents who had ignored me, who continued to ignore me.

I deserved more than that. I always had. It just took me a little while to realize it, and finally go after it for myself.

"I assumed you were either brave or stupid," Landon

said, still grinning. "I've decided on the former. You look like you're firing on all cylinders to me."

I laughed. "I'm just going to go ahead and take that as a compliment."

"You should. It was meant as one. I think you and Cash will get on just fine."

I had no idea how or why he thought this, since we'd just met and had talked for all of three minutes. But I'd take it, because I wanted that, too. More than anything.

"Do you know him well?" I asked, hungry for anything more he could share about the man I was marrying.

"Known him all his life. He's hard-working, honest, loyal." He looked at me, right in the eyes. His stare was earnest, unwavering. "Cash Smith is a good man. One of the best."

I drew in a shaky breath to steady my nerves. I knew these things. It had all been there in his emails. Not in a showy way. Just in the way he spoke about his day or his interactions with others.

I needed honest and loyal after the nightmare I'd been through with my ex-boyfriend, Keith. I swallowed as familiar fear sliced through me. He'd stalked and terrorized me when we broke up. Then things had escalated when he'd broken into my apartment in the middle of the night and threatened me with a knife.

To anyone who knew my history—and right now that was only the police investigating my case—moving here, doing this, would probably seem insane. But it felt the opposite to me. This was the clean break I so desperately needed. The new start. A way to build a beautiful new life on my own terms.

One night, I'd been sitting in the dark, too afraid to sleep, feeling lost, alone. Then I'd seen an advertisement in my Facebook feed asking if I'd love to live by the mountains. I'd clicked on it. I don't know why. I guess the picture of insanely beautiful snow-covered peaks had spoken to me. The link had taken me to FindMeAHusband.com. I'd seen Cash's *Wife Wanted* advertisement almost immediately.

And I'd just…known.

I wrote about romance every day. And I wanted that for myself. So I went after it. I made it happen.

A distant low hum echoed through the valley.

I searched the fields and hills surrounding us. "What is that?"

Landon patted my hand. "That would be your fiancé." He pointed up to the sky, to a speck in the distance.

"A plane?"

"Yep."

I squinted, my heart thundering harder. "*Cash* is in that plane?"

"He's flying it."

*Oh my God.*

I stared up at the sky, stunned. "He never said he could fly."

Landon chuckled. "Gotta keep some mystery in a relationship. Isn't that what they say? Besides, it's the only way to get to his property."

I spun to face him. "*What?*"

"He lives in a pretty remote area. You didn't know?"

I mean, kind of. I assumed he was an hour's drive from town or something when he said his place was isolated. But this was something else.

*Calm down. Nothing's changed. He lives a little farther out, that's all.* This was not a big deal. *Except for your total fear of flying, especially in small planes!*

"Where will he land?" I said, looking around frantically.

Landon pointed to a field. "There."

I shot to my feet as the small aircraft came in to land, bouncing and bumping along, with my heart in my throat the whole time. *Oh no. No, no, no, no.* That plane was small on a whole new *freaking* level.

It finally came to a stop. I stood there, wringing my hands as I took in the dark figure sitting inside.

Now my flying nerves morphed into something else. Cash was here. He was finally here.

I couldn't see him properly, since he was in shadow behind the window. When the door opened, those relentless nerves spiked so high my head spun.

One long leg appeared, then another, his massive thighs bunching as he climbed out. A navy thermal clung to his thick waist and flat stomach, molding perfectly to the jaw-dropping expanse of his colossal chest. And those shoulders? *Holy freaking hell.*

Then he was out, standing by the plane.

I took a startled step back, then stopped myself and quickly stepped forward, limbs shaky, heart pounding. My fiancé was...huge. A veritable mountain of a man.

He didn't look like his picture. Nope. Size aside—though I wasn't sure that was possible—in the photo he was clean shaven. The man walking toward me had a full beard and hair that needed a trim.

Landon muttered a curse beside me.

"That's...Cash?" I whispered, my throat suddenly closing up.

Landon laughed unsteadily. "Told the boy to shave."

*Boy?*

*Nope. Man.*

*All man.*

As Cash came closer his blue eyes hit me. They hit me *hard*, and I took another startled step back. His own step faltered, and he frowned, but he kept coming.

A hand was suddenly on my back, and I jumped.

"You keep backing up, honey, you'll end up rolling down the bank." Landon gave my shoulder a pat. "He's big. I get it. But I promise there's nothing but good in that boy."

Okay, this was happening. This was Cash. My Cash. The man who'd sent me all those beautiful emails. He was bigger than I'd imagined—*a lot bigger*—and there was the beard. I mean, it was nice. I actually liked it. I just wasn't expecting it, that's all.

I smiled, even as my hands shook from nerves and excitement. And okay, there might have been a little uncertainty as well.

Cash stopped in front of me, and I tipped my head back. All the way back. "Hi," I breathed. Yes, breathed.

"Riley?" he said in a voice so deep and rough, I was surprised the ground didn't shake beneath me. It was even deeper than I remembered.

My smile wobbled. "I'm...yes. Riley." My gaze roamed over the sheer length and breadth of his body and back up. "You're ah...bigger than I expected."

He grunted.

*Grunted.*

An awkward silence fell between us. *This is to be expected,* I reminded myself. I'd done a lot of research on these kinds of marriages. I'd talked to people who had done similar to what we were now. The website Cash had used had a lot of useful information on what to expect as well, and there was a database of couples, the successful marriages and the failures. Most were happy to talk and share their experiences and I had taken advantage of the opportunity. Awkwardness was completely normal. He was more than likely as nervous as me.

I beamed up at him, letting the warmth in my heart show on my face. Yes, it was a shock finally seeing him in person, but I was happy to be here. "I'm so excited to finally meet you...to *see* you in the flesh." Then I stepped closer and wrapped my arms around his thick waist, hugging him.

Cash tensed.

I waited for him to hug me back.

Landon cursed behind me.

Cash's arms stayed at his sides.

Was he disappointed? Was seeing me in person a letdown?

I pulled back, heat washing my face, and suddenly those massive arms came around me and tugged me closer. He patted my back awkwardly. Maybe it wasn't me? He lived alone. His house was remote. Way more remote than I originally thought. Maybe he wasn't used to physical contact? I guess having someone hug you when you weren't used to it could be jarring?

Then he pulled back and surprised me further by taking my hand.

He paused and glanced down, his thumb gliding over the ring he'd sent me, and he made a rough sound.

I followed his gaze, taking in the way his fingers were curled around mine, and bit my lip. My hand disappeared in his. His fingers were long and thick, the skin rough from a life of working with his hands. I imagined him typing letters to me, those thick fingers stabbing at the keyboard, and my smile widened.

"Let's go," he rumbled and headed for the general store.

I followed, not that Cash gave me much choice, his hand was still wrapped tightly around my own.

"What are we doing?" I asked when we walked into the store.

"Getting married."

"Now?" I mean, I knew it was happening today, but I assumed we'd talk for a while first, now that we were face to face.

"Won't be back for a month," he said, dropping my hand and pulling a piece of paper from the pocket of his jeans. He handed it to Landon. "Marriage license."

Landon nodded and smiled at me. "Let's get this done. You'll want to head out before it gets dark."

Cash grunted. Again.

"Um, this all seems..."

Cash looked down at me, his pretty blue eyes hitting mine with a force that made my knees almost buckle. He wanted this. He wanted me. It was all there in those expressive eyes. And just that look from him calmed me.

I glanced back at Landon. "You can perform weddings?"

"Yes, ma'am. Got ordained online. I'll send the paperwork in once you two sign it."

"Okay. Let's do this," I said, before I chickened out.

Cash tensed beside me, and I peered up at him again. He was staring at me with an intensity that stole my breath.

"Right, repeat after me. I, Cash Wyatt Smith, take you, Riley Emeline Lewis, to be my wife."

Cash repeated the words, all deep and rumbly, then Landon told him the next bit. Cash shifted, his wide shoulders straightening. "I promise to be true to you in good times and in bad, in sickness and in health. I will honor you all the days of my life," Cash repeated, eyes burning into me, face flushed.

I shivered. His voice. *Dear God.* I wasn't sure I'd ever get used to it.

"Put the ring on Riley's finger," Landon said.

Cash pulled a simple gold band from his pocket, took my hand in his, and slipped it on my finger.

"Now it's your turn," Landon said to me and rattled off what I had to say.

I glanced back up at Cash. His eyes bore into me so intensely that a shiver moved through my entire body. It wasn't a bad shiver. But I was freaking out just a bit. This quiet, intense man was about to become my husband. The man I lived with...slept with.

The nerves skyrocketed.

He squeezed my hand gently. "Riley?"

The way he said my name, unsure, softer, but no less rough pulled me from my mini freak-out. *This is what you want. This is why you're here. You know this man, you've been talking to him for months.*

You *know* him.

I'd known him the moment I'd stared into his eyes.

"I, Riley Emeline Lewis, take you, Cash Wyatt Smith, to be my husband. I promise to be true to you in good times and in bad, in sickness and in health. I will honor you all the days of my life."

His fingers squeezed again, this time more like a spasm, like he'd been surprised I'd actually said the words.

"Riley, put the ring on Cash's finger."

I blushed and quickly grabbed my bag from the shop counter where I'd put it and pulled out the ring box. I flipped it open and pulled out the wide gold band I'd chosen for him. Honestly, I should have cottoned on to the size of the man I was marrying when he emailed me his ring size.

Taking his huge, hot hand in mine, I pushed it on his long, calloused finger and smiled up at him.

"I now pronounce you husband and wife. Congratulations. Cash, you may kiss your bride."

Cash's gaze shot to Landon, then back to me, and color darkened his cheeks—what I could see above his beard, anyway. I turned to face him fully, more nerves erupting in my belly. He didn't make a move. He stood there frozen, looking down at me.

Landon chuckled. "Don't blame you for looking at her like a deer in headlights, boy. But you're gonna have to help her out."

Cash frowned at Landon.

"You'll need to bend down, son."

He turned back to me, paused a moment, then bent down. I gripped his arms and rose to meet him, lifting to my tiptoes.

His lips finally touched mine, soft and warm, and a spark shot through me so hard and fast, I had to cling to him tighter, digging my fingers into his monster biceps so I didn't fall to the floor in a heap.

His breath huffed out of his nose against my cheek, and without my say-so my tongue slid out to graze his upper lip. Cash jolted and lifted his head sharply, his eyes flashing.

Did he not like it? Was it too much, too soon?

Cash turned back to Landon. "License."

Landon was grinning again, so wide all I could see were teeth. Cash signed it, then he took my hand and tugged me forward, putting the pen in my hand. Not handing me the pen, but literally putting it in my hand and wrapping my fingers around it, all but signing for me.

I signed my name and looked up at Landon. "Thank you for..."

Cash towed me from the general store. "This all of it?" he said, motioning to the three suitcases holding all my worldly possessions.

"Yes."

He dipped his chin, picked up all three, and headed to the plane. Landon waved as I jogged after my new husband, trying not to trip over the uneven ground.

"See you in a month, Riley," Landon called.

Cash loaded my bags into the plane, then opened the door closest to me, gripped my hips, and lifted me like I weighed nothing. I did not weigh nothing. I had curves. Some would say I was overweight. I didn't care what anyone said. I had the same figure as my mother and her mother before that. There was no changing it, even if I wanted to. I didn't.

Next to Cash, though, I felt petite in a way I never had in my life.

He shut my door, walked around, and climbed in beside me. Without a word, he reached over to help me buckle up and placed a headset on me. He put on his own, and soon the plane roared to life and we started moving.

My hands curled into tight fists, and I was finding it hard to breathe again. "I'm not the best flier," I said into the headset. "I apologize in advance if I talk your ear off. I talk when I'm nervous."

He said nothing.

"Oh God." We bumped down the "runway," picking up speed, and I shrieked and clung to the seat.

Then we were lifting off.

My hand flew out, gripping Cash's forearm. He again said nothing as I clung to him like Velcro while he tried to fly the plane at the same time.

If I hadn't been terrified, I would have been embarrassed or at least appreciated the pleasurable zaps firing up my arm from that little bit of contact between us.

Instead, I squeezed my eyes closed and hung on to him for dear life.

## 2

## CASH

I SHUT off the plane and turned to my new wife.

She was smaller than I thought she would be.

She also liked to talk. A lot. Something I kind of already knew from the two phone calls we'd managed. Which was a good thing, I guess, since I didn't.

Her eyes were currently closed. They'd been closed nearly the whole flight, but the few times when she'd opened them, they'd sucked me right in, like she'd reached inside me and taken my gut in her dainty fist. That's how I felt when I looked at her. I thought that might be a good thing.

"You can open your eyes," I said.

She let out a long breath, her shoulders drooping, which caused her breasts to bounce and the unrelenting ache in my stomach, the throbbing of my groin, to increase. I ignored it. Which wasn't as easy as it usually was. Probably because I wasn't just looking at a photo of Riley this time; I was looking at the real thing—all soft and round and warm. She was so warm.

When she'd hugged me, when she'd lifted up to kiss me,

the heat of her body and the way her curves pressed into me was better than anything I could have imagined. And I'd imagined a lot. She wasn't an image in my fantasies anymore. She was real. And she was mine.

My gut did that gripping thing again. Yeah, I ached from wanting her to touch me again. I hurt so badly from it. And I wanted her to keep touching me. Riley—my *wife*.

Christ, she was beautiful. The most beautiful woman I'd ever seen. Her soft, wavy blond hair reached just past her shoulders, and when she closed her mouth, her lips were like a plump rosebud. Her eyes were wide and the softest, loveliest brown, and her nose was a cute little button.

She undid her seatbelt, and her hands were shaking.

Riley had held herself rigid during the flight. It was obvious she didn't like flying, she'd told me that, but she hadn't complained. Instead, she'd grabbed my arm; she'd clung to me. I'd liked that. A lot. Did that make me an asshole? Probably. Definitely desperate and pathetic.

But Riley was everything I'd hoped for. More.

And I'd thought about it a lot over the last ten years, what it would be like to have a woman out here with me. Someone to take care of me, like my mother had taken care of my father. Someone to cook for me, keep the house. A warm body to hold at night.

My gaze moved over her face again, lingering on her mouth, and I had to clear my throat when I remembered her little tongue sliding against my lip. I'd spent the whole flight thinking about her mouth, that kiss. And though it had just been a short one, not the kind I fantasized about, it had been the best thing that had ever happened to me. I wanted to kiss her again. I wanted to kiss her all the time.

I wanted to do a lot more than that.

*She's your wife. You can kiss her whenever you want.*

And I wanted. I wanted, badly.

"Cash?"

I jolted at my name on her lips, then heat hit my face. I'd been staring at her mouth.

She reached out, her hand on my forearm again, and those same zaps of electricity shot through me. I had to stop myself from leaning closer, from begging her to keep touching me. To never let me go.

Riley bit her lip, her brows lowering. "Are you...okay? I mean, you are happy, right? Happy that I'm here?"

My face grew hotter. I wasn't great with words. This was the longest time I'd spent alone with a woman who wasn't my mother. I didn't know what I was doing. Was I happy she was here? Happy didn't come close. But I was also out of my depth, aching for my sweet little wife and scared out of my mind that I'd mess everything up.

*Talk, Cash.*

"Yep."

*Idiot.*

That wasn't enough. But I didn't know what to say. I shoved my door open and grabbed her bags down, then rounded the plane and opened her door for her. I reached up, and she gripped my shoulders instantly as I caught her around the waist and lifted her down. I had to bite back a groan as her soft, full breasts pressed against my chest, her hips brushing mine as she slid down the front of me.

I grunted from the contact, then I blushed hotter. There was no way she didn't feel how stiff I was behind my zipper.

I winced and quickly put her on her feet, snatched up her bags again, and headed for the house. My nerves grew again as I led her up the front steps. I'd built this place just for me. My family home was on the other side of our property. I hadn't wanted to live there after my parents died—too many memories. I'd scattered their ashes there right after I lost them, and now the old place had been pretty much taken over by nature.

The house had been built by my great-grandparents and hadn't been in the best of shape when I was a kid. My dad and I had planned to build a new house together. We never got that chance.

The last time I saw it, a tree had taken out one wall and a family of raccoons had moved in.

My father would have liked that, giving that piece of our land back to nature.

This house was small: one bedroom, a living room, a kitchen, laundry, and bathroom. I was glad I had a working toilet now. At least there was that. But I wasn't finished. I'd begun working on an extension, adding another couple of bedrooms and an office for Riley to write her books in.

I switched off the small electric fence charger, unhooked the bungee cords across the door, unlocked it and shoved it open. She followed me in.

"What was that?" she asked.

"Electric bungee. Stops the bears."

She laughed nervously. "Bears. Right...of course. How could I forget?"

I strode through the living room and into the bedroom, putting her bags on the floor. My gaze moved to the bed, and my gut tightened, the ache increasing, becoming almost unbearable.

"This is so pretty," she said behind me.

I had to stop myself from jumping out of my skin.

"Still building the extension," I made myself say. I wanted her to know I was going to give her a good home, that I could provide for her. That I'd give her whatever she needed.

"So right now it's just the one bedroom?" she asked and glanced around my room.

Her cheeks were pink, her eyes wide. I cleared my throat. "Yep."

"Maybe you could...show me the rest of the house?"

Was being in the bedroom with me scaring her? The grip in my gut wasn't the good kind anymore. What if she didn't want me like that? What if she saw the size of me and was disgusted? Afraid?

My heart beat faster.

*She married you.*

I dragged in a breath, trying to calm myself. She had. She could have backed out, but she hadn't.

I dipped my chin and led her back into the living room, then through to the kitchen. I motioned to the door off that. "Laundry and bathroom. Just put them in."

She walked through, and I held my breath. Riley said she loved baths, so I put in a tub. It was the old, heavy, cast-iron, claw-foot kind. I'd taken it from my family home, the only thing I had here from my life before I lost my folks. It'd taken some getting it here because of its size and weight. I'd restored it for her, as a kind of wedding present.

She stood in the middle of the room and took it all in. It was a big bathroom. I'd built the cabinets and ordered the basin and toilet in special from the city. The washing machine was new, too.

"This is...*wow*, Cash, this is beautiful. If the extension you're working on is half as nice, your house is going to be gorgeous."

"Ours," I said before I knew the word was coming out of my mouth.

"Pardon?" she said, turning to me, eyes wide.

"Our home," I forced myself to repeat, even as my face heated again.

Her lips curled up at the edges. "Oh, yes. Ours."

I wanted to kiss her then, badly.

Instead, I walked out before I embarrassed myself.

---

WE'D FINISHED EATING A LITTLE WHILE AGO. I'D HAD SOME leftover venison stew I'd heated up. Riley was on the couch, her legs tucked up under her, eyes heavy. She was tired and trying to fight it.

It wasn't overly cold, but I'd lit the fire. I didn't want her cold. I wanted her to feel warm and happy here with me, safe. She needed to know how good I could take care of her.

It was getting late, but neither of us had made a move to the bedroom.

What was I supposed to do? Did she expect me to make the first move? How did I do that? Did she even want that? Did she want time to get to know me before we did...anything?

"I love the wedding ring you chose, and you know I adore my engagement ring," Riley said, breaking the silence and beaming at me, then glancing down at her hand. "I know I already emailed you that I loved it, but it really is perfect. I couldn't have chosen better myself."

I flushed with pleasure. I'd been terrified of getting it wrong. "Good," I choked out, my vocal cords feeling impossibly tight. I'd picked them out of a catalog Landon had ordered for me. The engagement ring had a diamond in it, was dainty and pretty like Riley, which is why I chose it.

I looked down at the one she'd slid on my finger earlier and swallowed, hard. I liked seeing it there. I liked the way it made me feel. Like I belonged to Riley. Like we belonged to each other. Insane, I know, since I could barely goddamn talk to her.

"I almost forgot. I have something for you," she said, breaking through the silence and my racing thoughts. She left the room and was back a few minutes later with a book. As she handed it to me, her face lit up in a way that stole my breath and made me nervous at the same time. "You said you liked thrillers. I bought you the new Stephen King."

How did she know I liked thrillers? Had I told her and forgotten? I didn't think so. I took it from her and frowned down at it.

"Um...is it okay if I take a bath?" she asked.

"Don't need to ask," I said roughly as images of Riley naked in the tub filled my head. "Towels are in there."

She started toward the kitchen.

"Thank you," I blurted. "For the book."

She smiled at me over her shoulder, then disappeared around the corner.

I wandered around the house, shaking out my hands, not sure what to do with myself. There was a restlessness inside me, something I'd never felt before. I gripped the back of my neck and dragged in a deep breath. It didn't help, nothing helped. And every now and then I'd hear a splash in the bathroom as Riley moved in the water. My imagination ran rampant. I may not have ever been with a woman, but I wasn't an idiot. I'd seen movies. I had a large DVD collection, and I obviously read books, lots of books.

The bathroom door lock clicked, and I froze in my position right beside it. I hadn't meant to move so close. She'd think I was listening on purpose. *You were.*

The door swung open, and Riley jumped, looking up at

me wide-eyed. She was wrapped in a damp towel. Which meant she was naked underneath. "Cash?"

"I-I was just..." What? I couldn't think of a good excuse.

She let out a shaky breath and winced, her cute little nose crinkling. "Look, I know things are...awkward right now. And Lord knows, I'm no expert. I wasn't around my parents enough to know what a healthy relationship looks like. But we know each other, we've talked over email for months. And I like you, Cash. I've grown to...care about you. A lot. We got married today." She smiled up at me. "But I'm so incredibly nervous. I don't know what to do or say. And I *think* you might be feeling the same way?"

I nodded, nostrils flaring, breathing in her scent, a scent unique to Riley, mixed with my soap. I barely stopped myself from leaning down and licking the drop of water sliding over one of her creamy, smooth shoulders.

She touched my arm, and I jolted. "Are you, Cash? Are you feeling the same way?"

She needed something from me, and I didn't know what to do, what to say. My inclination was to howl in frustration, but that would only scare her. So I went with the truth. "I'm not...great with words. I want you to feel..."

"Kiss me," she said.

I froze, *again*. "What?"

"I think we should just...get it out of the way, don't you? I know some couples in situations like ours wait before they start the...*intimate* side of their relationship. But I'm worried the longer we wait, the harder it'll get. What do you think?"

I wasn't thinking. Not one damn thought. All I could see was her pretty, rosebud lips. "Yep," I choked out.

"So you think we should...um, kiss?"

"Yep."

She moved closer, her face tilted up to me, waiting,

waiting for her husband to kiss her. I wanted to do this right. I didn't want to mess it up. *Do it, Cash. Kiss your damned wife.*

I thought about our short kiss at the general store, the way her tongue had darted out. How I wanted to sink into it, into her. I'd let nerves get the better of me then, and it was happening again.

Riley was right. I didn't want weeks of this tension. Of leaving it so long that it made things harder. I needed to do this now. I wanted to do this now.

She was a lot shorter than me, which made it difficult. If I was going to do this the way I needed to, and I had to, bending or crouching so much would make it more awkward. So instead, I gripped her hips over the damp towel and lifted her.

She made a little squeak sound, grabbing my arms, and I sat her on the kitchen counter in front of me.

We stared at each other.

I swallowed thickly.

"Cash?"

"I'm gonna kiss you now, Riley," I said like a damned fool.

She nodded, her gaze dropping to my mouth, then lifting back to my eyes. "Okay," she whispered.

That whisper lifted the hair on the back of my neck and made my gut ache on a whole new level. I shuffled forward and raised my hand to cup the side of her face. Her golden blond hair was soft and wavy, tickling the back of my hand.

My heart raced as I dipped my head and leaned in closer. Her knees pressed into my stomach, and my breath huffed from my nose as my cheek touched hers. Her hands settled on my shoulders, her fingers digging into the muscle, and I moaned.

I loved the way she gripped me, holding tight like she

had in the plane, using me to ground herself. She could use me in any way she needed. I was hers.

Amazingly, this beautiful woman wanted to kiss me—to be mine—and I'd give her everything she asked for.

I'd been alone—so lonely—for so damn long.

"Please," she said, her lips not quite touching mine yet.

My woman shouldn't have to beg for anything from me. Not one thing. So I turned my head the little bit needed and pressed my lips to hers almost as soon as the plea left her precious lips.

At that first gentle contact, I groaned. How could the simple act of touching lips be this good? Zaps of pleasure fired from that point of contact right to my chest, then raced through my gut and down to my groin.

Her fingers dug deeper, and I groaned again, my mouth, my body seeming to know what to do all on its own. My lips moved against hers, then parted, my tongue flicking into her mouth. Her sweet little tongue flicked out in return, tasting, testing.

She whimpered, and I—*snapped*.

My arms banded around her, and I lifted her off the counter, one arm under her round bottom, the other buried in her wild, blond hair at the back of her head. I tilted my head, my only thought to go deeper, to get more Riley. My tongue plunged into her mouth again, and she gave it back to me, her arms coming around my neck, holding tight.

My hand curled around her bottom—so much soft flesh —and my fingers squeezed.

She wriggled against me. "Cash," she whispered against my mouth.

Her scent filled my head, the softness of her lips, her taste, and that warmth—that perfect, intense warmth of her skin—soaked into me, deep, letting me know she was real, she was here with me, that I wasn't alone anymore. All of it kicked me low in the stomach.

*Oh Christ.*

I was going to come if I didn't stop this *now*.

I couldn't humiliate myself in front of my sweet, perfect, beautiful wife just from kissing and holding her.

Still, I couldn't stop myself from gripping her luscious bottom tighter and pressing her hips into mine, grinding against her, tempting fate. My cock started to pulse, and my balls drew up.

*No. Not like this.*

I tore my mouth from hers and sat her back on the counter, taking a quick step back. I was breathing hard, my fists clenched tight. I was in pain, so much pain, so desperate to pull her back into my arms, to rub against her some more, to reach down right in front of her and squeeze myself through my jeans until I came anyway, like the pathetic virgin I was.

"I-I'm sorry," I said so roughly she flinched. I took another step back, wanting to flee but knowing that was probably the worst thing I could do.

"Don't go," she said, like she could read my mind. "Please don't go."

## 3

### RILEY

Cash backed away while I sat there trembling, desperate for him to touch me again. "Cash?"

He took another step back. "I have to…" He turned and rushed out of the kitchen.

I jumped when the front door banged shut.

What the hell just happened? I was sitting there panting, body alive, electric. More turned on than I could ever remember being. And he couldn't get away from me fast enough. I'd never been kissed like that in my life. *In my life.* And I'd had my fair share of kisses. I mean, I'd had a handful of boyfriends. I'd gone to college and hooked up at parties.

The point was, I'd experienced some terrible kisses over the years. And some really good ones. But none had even come close to that.

Had I pushed for too much, too fast? Did he think I was a terrible kisser? Wasn't he attracted to me?

God, was he having second thoughts about the whole thing?

I couldn't go back to the city.

My belly churned as familiar fear worked through me. Clutching my towel to my chest, I climbed off the counter and walked through the living room on shaky legs. I moved to the window and stared out at a large barn in the field by the house. Light glowed from inside.

He'd run away from me.

Couldn't get away from me fast enough.

The backs of my eyes stung as the full weight of the day came crashing down. I was exhausted, emotionally and physically drained from the nerves and excitement...the uncertainty. I'd had a lot of rejection in my life, from the people who should love me the most. And Cash's rejection made the weight of it all too heavy to bear.

I bit my lip and rushed to the bedroom.

I quickly changed into my pj's and climbed into bed. Breathing deeply as I pulled the covers up to my chin, I tried with what little strength I had left not to cry. My belly churned in awful, relentless knots. What had I done? Had I made a huge mistake? I'd just married a man I hardly knew. What the hell had I been thinking?

I hadn't been. I'd gone with my gut instinct, and it had been loud. Thinking about Cash had made my world slow and calm when it had been a terrifying mess for so long. Looking at his picture, into the gentleness I'd seen in his beautiful blue eyes, had filled me with warmth.

Had made me feel—safe.

Cash had been so open with me in his emails, and now? Now he was so...closed off. Elusive.

I shut my eyes. After the day I'd had, I needed sleep, lots of sleep. So much had happened. But I had a horrible feeling that if I fell asleep with my emotions all over the place like they were, all I'd see were monsters. *A monster.* I couldn't handle the nightmares, not tonight.

A face flashed through my mind, one I'd been working hard to pretend didn't exist. Keith. I shuddered, chills dancing over my skin as my heart pounded along with remembered terror. I snuggled deeper under the covers. I was safe here. I was safe.

––––––––

THE BED SHOOK, AND I STARTLED AWAKE WITH A SCREAM.

"It's just me," Cash's deep voice said low through the darkness.

"S-sorry, I was just...I-I got a fright. I'm not used to...to sharing a bed." My heart raced a mile a minute. For a split second I'd been back in my apartment in the city, waking to a different man in my room. I shoved the image from my mind. Keith wasn't here. He'd never find me here.

*You're safe.*

Cash was silent for several long moments. "You want me to go?"

"No," I said too loudly, my hand shooting out and grabbing for him before he could leave me again. My fingers met hot, bare skin. A colossal pec to be exact. "I mean, no... please stay. I don't want to be alone."

I'd gone to sleep thinking things I didn't want in my head, remembering things that made my stomach revolt. What I needed was to feel close to someone. Not someone...Cash.

I'd wobbled earlier. I'd let the pain, the damage my parents caused sneak back in. And I'd doubted myself *and Cash*. We hadn't even spent a full day together. I needed to trust that we could work through this initial awkward part, that ahead of me was something beautiful.

I may not have known Cash long, and really only via

email, but since the first time he contacted me, I felt a connection to him. And that picture...I'd looked into his eyes and saw nothing but good. I was like my mother that way. The only good thing she'd ever given me. I just *knew* things. Call it a sixth sense, call it intuition—whatever it was, I'd always trusted mine, and it had always been right.

I'd ignored it once and I'd paid for it, was still paying for it.

I needed to trust my instincts now.

The mattress dipped as he settled back down.

I tried to see him through the shadows, but I could only see a faint outline. "I know I...I pushed you earlier, and I promise I won't do that again, but could you...would you hold me?"

He didn't answer with words but actions. One moment I was on my side of the bed, the next his big, strong hands, capable of building houses, of flying planes, of cupping the side of my face like I would break if he wasn't careful, were wrapped around me, tugging me across the mattress.

Then I was engulfed in heat as the solid wall of his massive body pressed against mine. He was wearing pants, flannel by the feel, and no shirt. The heat of his skin radiated from him, soaking through my pj's down to my bones.

He wasn't just holding me, this was the bear hug of all bear hugs. His strength and warmth engulfed me, was working through me, annihilating my demons, melting them away with every second of comfort he gave.

"I can't remember the last time I was hugged...can you?" I said into the darkness before I could think better of it.

"Yep," Cash said, surprising me.

"You can?" My hand was against his hot skin, and I couldn't help but stroke his chest. It was impossibly wide, strong, and muscled, and a little hairy. Not too much, but more than a dusting. I liked it. There was something comforting about it.

"Ten years."

My hand stilled. All of me stilled.

Cash made a rough sound, not actual words, but I was pretty sure he was telling me to keep petting him. I started again, and he sighed.

Relief washed through me.

"That's a long time," I said, stating the obvious.

"Yep."

"Was it with an ex-girlfriend?" We'd never really talked about past relationships. It was probably something we should have discussed. But we were trying to get to know each other, why would we waste precious time talking about a person who wasn't important anymore? Well, that was the reason I hadn't.

His arm spasmed around me. "My mom."

"I'm sorry," I said, my heart hurting for him. He'd shared that he'd lost them in one of his emails.

"It's okay," he said gruffly. "And you didn't," he said after a moment.

"I didn't what?"

He was quiet again. His heart raced faster against my palm. The sound of him swallowing convulsively reached me in the dark. "Push."

I pressed closer to him, I couldn't help it. His skin smelled amazing. Soap and pine and earthy man. "But you...you left, and I thought..."

"Didn't wanna disgrace myself," he bit out, voice tight.

I moved my hand to his bicep and gripped tightly, afraid he'd pull away or try to leave again. "You mean you..."

He swallowed again, thickly. "Yep."

"Oh." He was uncomfortable. I didn't want that. "We're

husband and wife. Granted the way we got here isn't the normal way of doing things, but I want us to start as we mean to go on. So in the spirit of honesty, I uh, was almost *there* myself."

His big body jolted. "What?"

"That kiss, Cash. I've never experienced anything like that. If you'd touched me, I could have...I would have, um... come as well."

Cash cursed and tightened his hold on me, like now he was afraid *I'd* run from him. Or God, maybe he was about to tell me something I didn't want to hear and was trying to cushion the blow.

I didn't know what he was thinking. He was impossible to read. Worst-case scenario, he wasn't feeling the way I was, amazing kiss aside, and he wanted to drop me off at the general store tomorrow and never look back.

"What's wrong?" I whispered, making myself ask. There was no missing the tension in his body.

"Need to tell you something," he rasped.

*Oh God.*

He made another rough, definitely angry, sound.

Now my belly was in knots again. "Did I...did I do something to upset you?"

"No," he said quickly. "Christ, no. Not angry at you, Riley...at me."

"Why?" Now my heart was racing as well.

"I didn't want to walk away, I ah...wanted to give you..." He cleared his throat. "What you needed, but I...I..."

"Cash?"

"Don't know how," he finished roughly.

"You don't know how?" I had to be hearing him wrong.

"I don't know...what to do."

He what? No. How could that be? "Are you saying, you've never had sex before?" His hold was a vise around me now.

"Lived out here all my life. Don't go to the city. Make runs to the general store. Do my deliveries. Come home." He was quiet for several long seconds. "I've never been with a woman, Riley, at all. At the general store, that was the first time I'd kissed anyone."

I didn't know what to say. I mean, I was shocked, and I hated that he'd been alone all this time, but I was also relieved. "That's why you left?"

"Yep."

"And you are...attracted to me?"

He made a low, growly sound. "Yep."

I relaxed, relief washing over me hard and fast. "Well, that's good, because I am most definitely attracted to you."

A pause. "You are?"

I wriggled, and Cash loosened his hold on me enough that I could lift my head and look into his eyes, eyes that showed me more than he knew. I smiled. "Yes." I touched his face, his soft beard. His eyelids drifted closed for a moment, then opened again. Moonlight from the window streamed in, showing me his pale blue irises that almost glowed in the dark. "You don't ever need to be embarrassed with me. We'll work it out, learn what we...um, like, together."

"Yeah?" he rumbled.

"Yeah." I brushed my thumb over his lips, they were firm yet soft, and caught his gaze again. "I really like your eyes."

His throat bobbed as he swallowed. "I like your mouth and your...your...everything," he said roughly.

His cheeks darkened. I could tell even with only the light of the moon. This was hard for him. I ran my fingers over his heavy brow. "I was so worried. I felt close to you after our emails, then today everything was...strained. I'm glad we talked."

His eyes bore into me like I was the most exquisite creature he'd ever seen. Like I was some new discovery. I guess I kind of was, in more ways than one.

"Can I kiss you again?" he rasped.

I grinned and nodded.

Those big fingers slid into my hair, and he tugged me down, his lips taking mine. There was no finesse, no thought, just pure feeling, and like the last time, electricity shot through my veins. I was lit up, on fire, ravenously hungry, and unable to get enough.

Cash's beard tickling my skin as his lips opened under mine, his tongue exploring every inch of my mouth. His hand moved over my back, then down to my butt, squeezing restlessly like he had in the kitchen. His other arm was around my upper back, holding me tight, pulling me closer.

I kissed him back just as fiercely, lost to sensation.

Sparks of pleasure shot through me, arrowing down between my legs, and I squeezed them together.

"Is this good?" he asked roughly.

"Yes, Cash, so good," I said against his lips. "Do you like it?"

He made an urgent sound that I took as a *yes*, as he gripped my butt tighter and ground his massive erection against my belly.

"Riley," he said desperately.

"It's okay," I whispered. "Do you want me to...to touch you?"

"Yes...no." He hissed. "I want to make you feel good. I want to make you come. Help me."

Oh God.

*Oh. God.*

I wanted that too. So much.

Taking his hand in mine, I pressed it low on my belly. "Put your hand down the front of my shorts, under my panties."

He shuddered, and I squirmed as the rough skin of his fingers grazed my belly as he hooked the elastic of my pj shorts, then my panties, and slid inside.

"Riley, Christ, so hot and slick and..." His hips jerked.

I covered his hand with mine, pushing it deeper in my panties as I lifted my knee, resting it on his hip to hold me wide. Then I took hold of his massive index finger and moved it where I wanted it. "If you rub my clit just right, you'll make me come." I dragged his finger through my juices, and the wide tip nudged against my opening.

His hips jerked again, and his big body trembled. "*Oh God, Riley,* you're...you're so small there...*oh fuck.*"

"Are you worried you won't fit?" I whispered.

He moaned, seemingly incapable of words.

"You're big, I can feel you against my belly. But we'll fit together just fine when we decide to take it there, I promise."

He shook harder.

I couldn't take another minute, I needed to come. I moved his finger up so it was at my clit. "You feel that? That little nub?"

He growled.

"Circle it for me, nice and slow, and I'm going to touch you at the same time, okay?"

"*Yes. Please*, touch me."

I shoved my hand down the front of his pajama bottoms. He wasn't wearing any underwear, and my hand met hot, hard flesh. He was as big as I thought. Bigger. I wrapped my fingers around his length, smooth and silky over molten hot steel.

"*Oh God. Oh God*, Riley."

He thrust into my hand, even as his finger continued working my clit. I was so wet, so desperate to come, all I could do was whimper as I stroked him faster.

"Tell me what to do," he choked out.

"Rub across it now. *Yes*...yes, like that." I was close, and I wanted him to come with me. "Am I...is this how you like it?" I asked him, wanting him to feel as good as me.

He thrust into my hand faster. "Do anything. You can do anything to me."

He rubbed me more firmly, picking up the pace, and I gasped for breath as pleasure built higher inside me, until I couldn't take it another moment. I threw my head back and cried out, coming against his fingers.

Cash stiffened, then jerked in my hand, groaning deep.

His face contorted with pleasure, with awe, as he came for me. His wide chest heaved, and he yanked me forward, plastering me against his chest, holding me so tight I could barely breathe, but I didn't care. What we'd just done was incredible.

"Did I...did I make you feel good?" he asked after a while of us both trying to catch our breath.

I nuzzled his chest. "Yes, you were perfect."

He rolled to his back, taking me with him, so I was plastered against his side. "I just want to take care of you, Riley."

Then his breathing evened out.

A moment later he was fast asleep.

I smiled against his side. I wanted to take care of him as well.

## 4

---

## CASH

I GLANCED at the house again. What was Riley doing right now? Something I'd been asking myself all day—the last few days. I scowled and hefted another plank of wood onto my shoulder. What had she done to me? I had a constant ache in my gut and a weird feeling in my chest.

I wanted to be inside the house with her. I'd brought her here for a lot of reasons: So I wasn't alone anymore. To make my life easier, better. So I could get more done around the place. So far, I'd barely done any of the things I needed to do around the property.

How could I when all I could think about was what we'd done in bed three nights ago? The way she'd touched me and let me touch her. Her sweet, hushed words in the darkness, the little noises she made when I used my fingers on her to bring her to orgasm.

The feel of her tight opening against the tip of my finger. I'd wanted to plunge inside so badly. A shudder wracked through me. She said we'd fit together just fine, but I wasn't so sure. What if I hurt her? She was so small. And what I wanted to do to her, the way I wanted to take her—

I clenched my fists and shook my head, trying to dislodge the images in my head of her under me, my hands holding her down while I slammed into her curvy little frame. *What the hell is wrong with you?*

Christ in heaven, I needed to stay the hell away from her. At least until I could gather some control. I needed to treat her with care, with respect. Not force her to endure my raw, unschooled hunger for her.

No, I hadn't been with a woman before, but I'd been imaging what it would be like for a long time. Someone to talk with, eat with, share a life with. Someone to sate this burning lust deep inside me.

So many nights I'd lain in bed, feverish with hunger, cock in hand, feeling so incredibly lonely, so desperate for another person to touch me. Someone to help relieve the unrelenting ache between my thighs. Someone to just...hold me. It had gotten so bad, the loneliness had nearly broken me.

Until I finally did what Beau had suggested during one of my deliveries to their homestead.

Advertise for a wife, like he had.

I'd used the computer at the general store and started my search. Since I'd needed Landon's laptop, I'd had to share what I was doing. He'd ended up helping me communicate with Riley. I didn't have a computer, so I'd call him via satellite phone, he'd read me her emails, and I'd tell him what to reply with.

It was awkward and time consuming, but it was worth it.

Now I had my perfect, little wife. So beautiful and sweet. I wanted to protect and look after her. And fuck her so hard the walls would shake. If I took her like I desperately wanted to, she'd never look at me the same again. She'd probably run from me and never look back.

I couldn't have that.

I finally had everything I wanted.

I couldn't lose her. Not now.

Which was why I was getting up before she woke and climbing into bed after she was asleep.

I'd had her here less than a week, and I was already ruining everything.

I glanced at the house again and bit back a curse as a wave of lust hit me so strong I had to lock my knees. She was inside. In *my* house. Mine.

She was mine.

Growling, I dragged a hand down my beard. I'd woken early this morning with her plastered to my side—her arm flung over my stomach, her knee bent, thigh over mine, her face pressed against my ribs—and a cock so stiff I'd barely stopped myself from rolling her to her back, shoving her thighs wide, and stuffing her full.

Which was why for the third morning in a row, I'd gently shifted away from her and snuck out before she woke, busying myself milling wood for the house extension. Riley hadn't sought me out. Not once.

I was confused and angry with myself. I didn't know what to do.

My stomach rumbled. I'd barely eaten, and I was tired. I wanted her. I wanted to make things right between us. How did I do that?

My stomach rumbled again. It was getting late. The sun lower in the sky. Time to eat. *You need to go inside. You're making everything worse.*

I couldn't avoid her anymore. What kind of a man avoids his wife?

*One with no self-control.*

Somehow, I had to ignore the rough need I had for her.

Not easy with her in my bed every night, curled up beside me, wrapping herself around me even in sleep.

Though, two of those nights, she'd woken with a scream, and as soon as I'd muttered what I hoped were soothing words, she'd curled into me and gone back to sleep.

I didn't know what caused her distress, but I liked that I was there to comfort her.

It was the sweetest torture.

I adjusted the planks of wood on my shoulder and headed for the house, carrying them around the back, ready to use in the morning. I was hot, sweaty, hungry, and desperate to see Riley when I walked in. To try to make amends for the way I'd been behaving.

But when I stomped in, she wasn't in the living room or the kitchen. I strode to the bedroom, then the bathroom.

She wasn't there, either.

I stood there, looking around my small cottage like I expected her to appear out of nowhere.

Every muscle in my body locked tight. *Has she left? Has she left me?*

I ran out the door, searching the fields around the house—

A foot poked out from behind a tree.

My heart kicked into action, and I strode toward it—her —with what felt like a boulder in my throat, gut in knots. Of course, she hadn't left.

*She has no way to leave.*

I shook that thought away.

*She married you. She wants to be here.*

Still, that moment of fear that she'd fled from me had me barking out her name, "Riley."

Her foot jolted, then her head appeared around the side of the tree. "God, Cash, you startled me."

I'd startled *her*? She'd scared the hell out of me. "What're you doing out here?" I inwardly winced at the growl in my voice but couldn't seem to stop myself.

She frowned and lifted the laptop on her lap. "I was writing."

I dragged in a rough breath, feeling like an idiot, my heart still not calm, and there was no reining it in. "I'm hungry."

*What the hell is wrong with you?*

Riley's mouth opened. Closed. "Um, I'm sorry, I didn't think...I..." She stood so quickly she nearly fell over. My hand shot out, steadying her, and just that tiny bit of contact with her warm, smooth skin against my palm and I was fighting not to snatch her up, shove down her pants, and take her against the tree she'd been hiding behind.

I pulled my hand back and shook my head. "I didn't mean..."

"No, you're right. You've been outside working all day. And I guess that was part of the deal, right? Me cooking the evening meals."

*The deal?*

I hated that. This wasn't some *deal*. She was my wife.

I couldn't have messed this whole thing up more if I'd tried. "Riley..."

"Sorry, when I write I can get caught up and lose track of time. And honestly, since I haven't seen you in days, I didn't think... I'll make something now, while you clean up."

She wasn't looking at me. Why wasn't she looking at me. "Riley?"

But she was already striding back toward the house, shoulders stiff, chin high, and even with my total lack of experience with people, I didn't miss she was angry. Maybe even hurt.

Her round bottom twitched in her jeans as she walked up the steps and into the house, and I cursed loudly. I hadn't thought this through, any of it. Only about myself. My comfort. My feelings. I'd wanted someone to look after me, keep me company. Someone to share my nights with, to slake this burning lust inside me that...hell, that had started to scare me.

I hadn't thought about her.

Never about how she'd feel.

I was a selfish bastard.

Riley had feelings and emotions. I'd come all over her hand three nights ago, then avoided her. And when I'd finally seen her again properly, to talk to her, I'd demanded she cook me dinner.

If my cousins Beau and Hank were here, they'd be shaking their heads at me for acting like an idiot.

I started back toward the house, not knowing what to do or say. I wasn't used to talking, let alone soothing a woman's hurt feelings. She had a good reason to be angry at me, and I got the feeling I'd make her angry again over the next few months, since I was a goddamn clueless idiot.

*If she stayed that long.*

The ache in my chest increased.

I walked into the kitchen. Riley was chopping carrots. *Loudly.*

"Riley?"

"I'll be as quick as I can, Cash. And sorry, no chocolate cake tonight."

Yep, she was angry. No, furious. I frowned. "Cake?"

"It is your favorite, right? It was remiss of me not to have made you one by now. Please accept my apologies."

I frowned harder. When had I mentioned chocolate cake being my favorite?

I shook away that thought. She sounded different. Her voice was sharper. And I may be clueless and miss a lot, but I knew what sarcasm was. How could I not with Beau as a cousin? I'd screwed up. Badly. I'd been around my cousins and their wives enough to know when a woman was upset.

I remembered the sounds she made when I used my finger on her clit, when she came for me. She'd been happy then. She'd clung to me, snuggled closer. She'd liked that, too, snuggling. She'd stayed pressed up to me like that all night, had done it every night since, even if she was asleep. She'd smiled at me as well.

Would that make her happy again now? My gaze dropped to her round bottom, the way the denim hugged tight, the way the seam skated between her rounded cheeks, down farther, curving around between her thighs, along her pussy, and I licked my lips.

Would she like it if I used my mouth on her there? I'd seen it in movies, read about it in books. My mouth started to water. Or would she be disgusted?

She opened one of the cupboards under the sink, bending over and pulling out a pot.

"I know what I want...for dinner." My face exploded with heat. Had I actually said that out loud?

She turned to me, eyes flashing, a look on her face my mom had aimed at my dad many times when he'd said something stupid...but then Riley stilled as her gaze moved over my face, when she looked into my eyes.

"What do you want for dinner?" she asked, and her voice had gone husky.

My gaze dropped to the juncture of her thighs before I could stop myself, and I didn't miss her sharp intake of breath.

*Idiot.*

"I'm...I'm sorry," I bit out.

She put her knife down and turned to face me properly. "What are you sorry for?"

I shook my head, trying to find the right words. "This isn't a deal, Riley."

She took a step closer. "No, it's not. Are you really mad because I lost track of time and didn't make dinner?"

I shook my head. "With myself."

"For avoiding me for the last three days?"

I planted my hands on my hips to stop from reaching for her. "Yep."

"And you want to apologize?"

"Yep," I choked out. Why did I find this so damn hard?

"And how did you want to do that?" she said, her face pink, her beautiful eyes bright.

My gaze dipped again before I could stop it, struggling for control. "I-I'll make dinner," I said, trying to cover for what I'd almost given away. The dirty things I wanted to do to my perfect, new wife.

She tilted her head to the side. "No, I don't think that's what you had in mind."

I swallowed audibly.

"Tell me, Cash, tell me what it is you really want?"

I shook my head, feeling cornered. Embarrassed. Ashamed.

"Have you been thinking about what we did my first night here?" she asked, her lovely round breasts shaking slightly with her quickened breaths.

I hadn't seen them bare yet. I hadn't touched them. An image of them swaying as I pounded into her fired through my head, and it was my turn to suck in a breath.

"Or something else?" she carried on. "Are you hungry for *me*, Cash? Is that what you meant?"

I growled.

Like an animal.

Her eyes widened, lips parting. Her tongue swiped over her upper lip. "Do you want to use your mouth on me, Cash?"

I shuddered fiercely enough there was no way Riley missed it. "I'm sorry," I said again, embarrassed that I didn't know what to do. What the hell to say.

"Is that it? Is that what you want? You want to make me come with your mouth?" she asked again, her voice soft, sweet, quietly demanding an answer from me.

I started to shake my head.

"Tell me." There was a desperation in her voice that made me shake harder.

I was so hard now I hurt. I hurt so bad. I shouldn't say it. I shouldn't tell her what I was thinking, but right then I couldn't stop myself because Riley didn't look horrified. No, she looked—excited.

"I...I..." I cleared my tight throat. "I want to tear off those fuck-me jeans, lay you on the dinner table, and feast on your..." I swallowed audibly. "Your...pussy."

I stood there, breathing roughly, terrified she'd be disgusted by what I'd said yet desperate for her to want that, too. For her to want my mouth on her.

Her delicate nostrils flared, and she took another step toward me. "I'm glad you told me, Cash. Now come and get your reward."

My control crumpled.

With a vicious growl, I closed the distance between us, snatched her up into my arms, and strode the four steps to the table. I laid her back in the next breath, my hands tearing open her jeans, then yanking them and her panties down her legs.

No more panties. Riley should never wear panties. She should always be bare.

I sat heavily in the chair at the head of the table, gripped her ankles, dragged her toward me, then flung her legs over my shoulders. She laughed, and it sounded like lots of tiny bells, high and joyful.

I wanted to look up, to see that kind of joy on her beautiful face, but I couldn't look away from my prize. My *reward*. She was so pretty, pink and wet. She looked soft, was so incredibly soft there. I couldn't hold back another moment, and I buried my face where I wanted to be so badly I was certain I'd die if I didn't taste her.

She was warm and silky, and salty sweet.

She was perfect and precious.

I gripped her thighs harder, and damn near whimpered as I swept my tongue through the center of her, the same place where she'd guided my fingers last time. I flicked my tongue over the little nub that had made her come for me, her clit, knowing if I moved my tongue over it, if I kissed and licked and sucked, I could make her come again.

But I wanted to explore first. I traced the delicate, slick folds of her pussy, and worked my way down to her opening, dipping the tip of my tongue inside. *Oh God*. So good.

Riley gasped, and her fingers threaded through my hair, fisting. I liked that. And she seemed to be enjoying what I was doing, but I needed to be sure.

"You like that, darlin'?" I don't know where the endearment came from, but it felt right.

She gasped. "Yes...don't stop."

Stop? I never wanted to stop. I wanted to stay right there. My mouth pressed up against her pretty pussy, her taste on my tongue, her scent filling my head. Knowing that I was giving her pleasure filled me with pride. With happiness. Made me even harder, when I thought that was impossible.

If I could make her feel good like this all the time, maybe she wouldn't leave me. Maybe she'd stay. Maybe she'd overlook my constant inability to know the right thing to do or say.

I teased her tight opening again. Releasing one of her rounded thighs, I rested my finger right there, gently circling, pressing against it, sliding over the spot I wanted inside so badly.

"Please," Riley gasped.

"You want me to push inside, darlin'?" I choked out.

"Yes, *God yes*."

*Oh Christ*. On a broken curse, I slid my finger into her hot, tight heat and had to drop my other hand between my thighs and squeeze. I groaned as I dragged my finger out and pushed back in, mimicking what I wanted to do with my heavy, throbbing cock. It was like molten steel trying to burst through the front of my pants.

I was burning up. Burning for her.

I thrust in and out faster, my tongue sliding over her clit. Riley gripped my hair tighter, crying out, and wiggled her hips, pushing up against my mouth. She wanted more. I slid my finger out and pushed back in with a second one, my breath shuddering out of me when she arched and moaned, spreading her thighs wider.

I gripped my cock through my pants harder and wrapped my lips around her dainty clit and sucked.

"Cash, oh God. *Oh God*."

Her lovely round bottom lifted off the table, the muscles inside her clenching tight around my fingers, then releasing, over and over.

She screamed, and my gaze snapped up to her.

"Am I hurting you?" I started to pull back, horrified.

She shook her head frantically and kept hold of my hair, grinding against my face. "*Don't stop!*"

I groaned again, in relief, in pure pleasure. I'd done this. I'd made her feel this good. I'd made her come so hard she'd *screamed*. I didn't stop. I sucked her clit, lapped at it gently as she jolted and twitched, as her pussy continued to grip and release my fingers, until she stopped tugging my hair and collapsed back, limp and, hopefully, well satisfied.

Pressing kisses to the soft skin of her inner thigh, I continued working myself with my hand, unable to look away from her.

"I can't believe you've never done that before," she said, panting and blinking down at me.

The pride filling me spread. "It was good?"

She sat up, a smile on her beautiful face. "You doubt it? It's never been that good. No one else has ever made me come that hard."

My hand stopped working my cock, and my gut twisted. I didn't like that. I hated that. I drew in a rough breath as anger at the faceless men who had touched my wife, who had made her come, who had been inside her, fired through me. "Don't...don't talk about other men, Riley. I don't want to think about anyone else touching you."

I wanted to hunt them down and hurt them.

She scooted closer and cupped my face with both hands, brushing her thumb over my beard. "You have nothing to worry about. I promise."

She glanced down to where my hand still rested over the thick ridge of my erection and licked her lips. Shimmying forward, she climbed off the table, moved in between my spread thighs, and dropped to her knees.

"Darlin'?" I choked out.

She popped the button of my pants and peered up at me, a sexy, wicked smile on her lips. "It's my turn for a reward, don't you think?"

## 5

## RILEY

I took in the fierce need in Cash's eyes and had to pull in a steadying breath.

This massive, silent, intense man confused the hell out of me. He also turned me on like I'd never experienced.

I'd pushed him for more after our first kiss three days ago, and he'd withdrawn, and there I was doing it again. But I couldn't help myself. I didn't know what he was thinking, why he'd been avoiding me, but I'd made the decision to let him come to me when he was ready. I'd needed him to decide what he wanted. And honestly, I couldn't take more rejection, not from Cash.

I slid down his zipper and had to bite my lip when he froze, when the huge man looking down at me went rock solid, holding his breath as I revealed what he had underneath.

His long, wide fingers curled and uncurled at his side, an unmistakable tremble to them that made my heart ache and my body sing.

I'd seen him standing in the dark by the barn, gazing back at the house every night the last few nights.

And I'd lain there when he finally slid into bed late, when he'd drawn me close, thinking I was asleep. His deep sigh brushing my hair. The pounding of his heart thudding against my cheek.

He wanted me. I didn't doubt that. But it was obvious communicating what he wanted wasn't easy for him. I thought of his emails and shook off the fear in my belly, that maybe I'd been wrong, that he wasn't the man I'd thought he was, the man I'd grown to care about—that he might never let me in.

*It's only been four days.*

This was all new to him—the relationship, the sex. He just needed time, that's all.

I slid my hand inside his pants and took his incredibly hard cock in my hand. He was thick and long and veined. The skin was tinged purple, the head an angry red, and pre-come leaked in a steady stream from the tip. No, there was no mistaking how much he wanted me, at least like this.

I gave him a slow stroke. He had his eyes squeezed shut, teeth gritted, sweet agony lining his face. "Look at me," I whispered.

His eyelids snapped open, those bluest of blue eyes locking with mine. Eyes that showed me right to the gentle, kind soul of him. As always, they drew me in, that sense of rightness moving over me, that I was where I was meant to be.

My safe harbor.

The family I'd never had and so desperately wanted.

"You're hurting, aren't you?" I whispered.

Teeth still gritted, he dipped his chin.

"You're beautiful here, did you know that?" I said, stroking him again, telling him the truth. His thigh muscles bunched, going rock hard. "You're beautiful everywhere. So strong. So big. You can protect me, can't you, Cash? You'll always protect me?" The words came from deep inside me. Needy. Weak. But I'd been afraid for so long.

I'd let insecurity overtake the last few days, and I needed reassurance from him. I hated that I did, but I needed it more than anything.

He lifted a hand, cupping the back of my head, and his gaze penetrated mine even deeper. "Yes."

One word, just one, but said with a fierceness, a conviction that made it impossible to not believe him.

His gaze turned searching, and I quickly looked away. I didn't want to talk about the reason those words had been torn from me. I wanted to make my husband feel good, feel wanted. So instead of avoiding me tomorrow, he'd seek me out. Instead of my second-guessing what he needed, he'd ask.

Take.

I shivered and leaned in, dragging my tongue over the head of his cock.

"*Oh Christ.*" He slapped a hand down hard on the table as the fingers of his other hand tangled in my hair. "Do that again...please, darlin'?"

I did, and he jolted.

"How many times have you fantasized about this?" I asked, then licked him again.

His nostrils flared. "So many."

I tilted my head back and sucked the head into my mouth, swirling around it with my tongue. Cash made a broken sound that tore through my heart. Sweat beaded his forehead, and his entire body trembled.

I didn't want to tease him. I wanted him to let go. I wanted to drive him to stop fighting it, because he was. Something was holding him back, when what he wanted was the complete opposite. So I didn't toy with him, I gave the tip another swirl, then sucked him back, taking him as deep as I could while using my tongue to apply pressure.

He was far too big to take all of him, so I gripped the base and stroked him in time with my mouth, never taking my eyes off his face.

Cash cursed, and his massive thighs spread wider. "You're so beautiful, Riley. My wife's so beautiful. I don't deserve that pretty, rosebud mouth on my cock." He hissed and fisted my hair tighter. "You make me want so many...bad things. So many."

His other hand left the table and slid down my back, and because he was so much bigger than me, he barely had to lean forward to grip my butt. He squeezed convulsively, hard enough to leave a bruise. I moaned in pleasure.

He'd talked more the night we'd made each other come in his bed. And he was doing it again now. The only time he said what he was feeling was when he was losing control. His words echoed through my mind, but then vanished as Cash reached around and pushed two fingers inside me.

I moaned around his cock, stroking and sucking harder, faster as I cradled his balls in my other hand and massaged. Cash barked out a rough curse and shoved his fingers deeper inside me, pumping fast, staying deep.

I was going to come again.

I'd squeezed my eyes closed, and when I opened them, our gazes clashed. A rush of liquid heat slid from me, and I sucked him harder, watching as pleasure pain stole his features as he gasped for breath. Something moved through his eyes, dark, beautiful, something that had my inner muscles clenching down on his relentless, thrusting fingers.

Something I wanted more of.

"Gonna come," he barked out.

I stayed where I was, taking that big cock into my mouth over and over. He gasped, and I groaned around him, my eyes nearly rolling back as I came, gripping and releasing his fingers, rocking against his hand. Cash fisted my hair in a punishing grip, holding me on his cock as he shot into my mouth.

His loss off control just made me come harder. I swallowed him down, giving him what we both wanted, needed. His cock in my mouth, thick fingers buried in my pussy, the look in his eyes as he watched me—awe, affection, pure lust—I'd never felt so precious, so wanted. Not ever.

I licked and sucked him until he began to soften. When I finally released him, I rested my hands on his knees.

I smiled up at him. "That was...amazing."

He didn't speak. I didn't expect him to. Instead he caught me under the arms and lifted me, putting me in his lap and burying his face against my throat, still breathing heavily.

"Thank you," he said roughly.

Cash wasn't just thanking me for the blow job. He was happy I was there.

He wasn't the only one.

---

I WENT TO SLEEP THAT NIGHT CUDDLED UP TO CASH BUT WOKE a couple of hours later when the nightmares crept back in. I was back in my apartment, waking and realizing I wasn't alone. Thankfully, I hadn't let loose a scream this time. I'd snuggled closer to Cash and managed to go back to sleep. Something that never usually happened.

The second time I woke was when Cash slid his hand down the front of my pj shorts. It was a *much* better way to wake up, and I returned the favor, stroking him until he shuddered and came, then fell back to sleep. And the *last* time I woke was to the repetitive bang of hammering, and I was alone.

Now I was in the kitchen, pouring myself a cup of tea. I glanced up when Cash walked in. He was wearing worn jeans that clung to his long, solid legs and strained over his massive thighs. And a red thermal was molded to his chest.

He pushed his hands into his pockets and looked at me from under his thick black lashes. "Morning."

I grinned at him. "Morning...again," I said, unable to resist the reminder of the way he'd woken me earlier.

His cheeks reddened. "I'll be leaving soon. Deliveries."

I straightened. "Deliveries?"

"I need to pick up supplies from the general store and drop 'em off to some of the isolated properties."

"In your plane?"

"Yep."

I mean, I knew he made his living doing deliveries, but up until a few days ago, I'd assumed it was in a truck or something. "I thought you weren't going back for a month?"

He rubbed the back of his neck. "I go when I'm needed."

"You'll be gone all day?"

His body went rigid, like he'd tensed every muscle. "A night, maybe two."

"What?" My heart thumped harder. There was no hiding the horror in my voice. I didn't want to be here alone. I didn't want to be here without Cash.

He frowned, obviously surprised by my reaction.

"Can I go with you?"

His gaze slid down to my mouth. "Lots of flying."

He'd picked up on my fear, obviously. I'd rather that than be here alone with my own thoughts. I knew myself. The memories would overtake until my mind had me hearing things, seeing things. I wouldn't sleep. I'd lie there frozen in terror.

"Is there any other reason, besides my fear of flying, that you wouldn't want me to go with you?"

He shook his head.

I released a relieved breath. "Okay, I'll pack for a couple of nights, then?"

His color was high again, and under that beard his lips had curled up. He was happy I was going with him.

"Leaving in twenty," he said, then headed back outside.

I quickly packed, and when I went outside a short time later, Cash was walking around the plane, checking things off on a list. I didn't want to interrupt while he was so focused, so I stood back and waited. One of those large, rough-skinned hands swallowed the pen he clutched as he jotted something down. My gaze moved across his shoulders, over his back, and down to his thick, muscled behind. I shivered.

I'd never seen a man like him. Cash was built like a warrior from medieval times.

He glanced up when he finished, and there was no missing his surprise. He hadn't seen me walk out, he was so engrossed in his task.

"What were you doing?" I motioned to the list in question.

"Preflight checklist." Reaching through the open door of the plane, he tucked the clipboard holding the list into a pocket behind his seat, then came to me and took my bag, putting it in as well.

I moved closer to him. I always wanted to get closer to him. "So how many properties are we delivering to?"

His gaze slid to me, then down to my mouth. "Four."

I licked my lips, and his gaze grew intense. Suddenly, I

wanted to climb my mountain-sized husband and kiss the hell out of him. Somehow, I resisted. "I know it's a paying job, but are some of these people your friends?" I was curious. I wanted to see him with people he was close to, people he had an actual history with.

His forehead puckered. "Yeah. And the last drop-off is for my cousins, Beau and Hank."

"Oh, really? So I'll get to meet some of your family?"

He dipped his chin again. "Their women and kids as well."

Now I was really looking forward to the trip, despite the flying. "So both Hank and Beau have wives?"

"Yep," he said absently, still walking around the plane checking things.

I followed. "What are their names?"

"Hank's woman is Birdie. Beau's, Freya."

I had no idea what Hank and Beau were like, but if they were anything like Cash, maybe these women had some insight they'd be willing to share on how to deal with my gruff, uncommunicative husband. "What are they like?"

Cash stilled and frowned, like he'd never considered it. "Nice."

*Nice.* That was it. Good Lord, the man was impossible to get talking. Except, of course, when we were enjoying each other's bodies.

Then he turned to me again, that frown still there, and surprised me by expanding on that one word. "And they love cooking for their husbands."

I narrowed my eyes at him, and he *grinned*. I nearly fell over. He was teasing me, turning our fight into something we could laugh about. My heart exploded in my chest from the sheer pleasure of it. And holy hell, he was beautiful when he smiled, flashing his straight, white teeth, his eyes lighting up and softening all at the same time.

"*Har har*, and too soon, Mr. Smith. Too damn soon," I said, but I was pretty sure there was no hiding how breathless I sounded.

And then he went and chuckled, and I thought I might actually pass out.

"How did they meet?" I asked when I'd shaken off the shock of hearing that low, raspy, incredibly sexy sound. "Your cousins and their wives?"

"Birdie got lost on the mountain. Hank found her."

He moved to the other side of the plane, and I followed again. "And what about Beau and Freya?"

His gaze flicked to me. "Like us."

"Online?"

"Yep."

"Is that where you got the idea from?"

"Yep."

Now I *really* wanted to meet these women. "How long have they been together?"

"Few years."

*Wow.* I liked this. A lot. "Do they have kids, as well?"

His gaze flicked to me again. "Yep."

I tucked my hair behind my ear. "Do you think you'd want kids one day?" This was probably something I should have asked him before we got married. I mean, I'd wanted my own family forever. I'd been alone most of my life, sent away to school so my parents could travel without me getting in the way. But the family I craved didn't necessarily mean children. My parents had been terrible, and the idea of raising children kind of scared me.

He straightened, his eyes moving over me, my breasts, my belly, back up, and his nostrils flared. "Yep."

*Okaaaay*. My heart was racing again. "How many?"

"Three."

No hesitation. This was something he'd definitely thought about.

He moved toward me, and I tilted my head back and my heart raced even faster. Then his hands were on my hips and he was lifting me up, planting me in my seat. He didn't let go right away, kept his hands there, gently squeezing and releasing, his gorgeous eyes locking with mine. "You want kids?"

I swallowed, my mouth suddenly bone dry. "I-I'm fine, either way."

And that was the truth. I wasn't closed off to the idea. And maybe having kids with Cash would be amazing. He certainly wouldn't abandon his children, I knew that much. He gifted me with another smile, a smaller one this time but no less devastating, and shut my door.

When he climbed in I asked, "And when do you want these kids?"

Now I was thinking about how we'd make these babies. We hadn't had sex yet, and all of a sudden, I really, *really* wanted to, to the point that I was squeezing my thighs together. I mean, not the making babies part, not yet, but I was good with lots of practice.

He glanced at me, and his gaze moved over me again, hot and intense. He was thinking the same thing. It was there in his gaze. "No hurry."

I let out a relieved breath as he leaned over and helped me buckle in like he had the first time I was in here with him. Only this time he didn't shy away from touching me. No, his long, thick fingers grazed my arm, and as he pulled the straps over my shoulders his knuckles brushed the tops of my breasts. But he didn't stop there. He then dragged his hand down the strap, skimming over my now hard nipple and down to the juncture of my thighs to lock it in place.

I sucked in a sharp breath and squeezed my thighs together again.

Cash made a low sound but didn't look at me, or touch me more. He put my headset over my ears, then straightened, put on his own headset, and started the engine. I concentrated on breathing through the confusing feelings of fear and intense lust as we started moving.

"Okay?" he asked roughly.

"Yes. I know you'll keep me safe," I said again without thought but believing it with everything in me.

We barely knew each other, but in that, I had no doubt.

He'd keep me safe.

I also knew he needed me as much as I needed him. Cash had been lonely out here by himself. Anyone could see that. And I was determined to give him everything he needed and more. To nurture this connection between us.

Maybe his family could help me on that front? I had no idea how to get through to him.

I wanted my husband to let me in, and I'd do whatever it took to make that happen.

## 6
___

## CASH

WE'D BEEN to the general store and loaded the plane with supplies. Landon and Riley had talked, free and easy, like they'd known each other for years, and I hadn't liked it. Christ, I'd been jealous. I wanted to be able to talk with her like that, and I couldn't goddamn do it.

Yeah, we had talked a little more since we left home, but not like that. There was an easiness between her and Landon, an easiness I craved but couldn't find. I glanced at her again as we were coming in to land at our third drop-off and swallowed hard. Ever since we'd talked about kids all I could think about was planting a baby inside her. Riley all soft, her belly round.

I scowled. *What is wrong with you? You can barely talk to her*. We hadn't even had sex yet and already I was thinking about her carrying my babies. But good Christ, something about the sweet girl beside me brought out the caveman in me.

Riley closed her eyes as we headed for the runway, a flat-ish field near the cabin we were stopping at to deliver food and fuel.

Seeing her scared like that was a punch in the chest. "Hold on," I said, trying to gentle my voice. "This one's bumpy."

She scrunched her face up, squeezing her eyes tighter. As we touched the ground, her hand shot out again, like it had the first time—like she had when we landed at the general store earlier that day and the two stops after that— seeking comfort from me. I liked that she did that. Liked it more than was reasonable.

*I know you'll keep me safe.*

Her words from earlier had been on repeat in my head as well. And hell, if it was possible, I'd fly the damn plane with her in my lap. There was nothing I wanted more than her soft warmth wrapped around me, holding her tight, making sure she never felt scared again.

We bumped and jerked as we taxied down the field, and Riley's fingernails dug into my skin, adding more tiny crescent moons to the others she'd given me today. I liked that, too. I liked that she marked me while she used me to ground herself, that I'd be able to look down and see those marks for days to come and know that she'd sought me out when she needed me.

We stopped, and she finally opened her eyes, her entire body relaxing.

"Okay, darlin'?" The endearment had been slipping out more often, but still my face predictably heated. I blushed easily, and it was pissing me off.

She released a long breath and nodded, a small smile playing at the corners of her mouth. I wanted to kiss her. "Yes, I'm fine. But I don't think I'll ever get used to it."

"You will." I hoped so, anyway. She hadn't wanted to be left behind, and I hated the idea of being apart from her.

Tucker walked out of his workshop by the house and

strode toward us. I climbed out, then came around and opened Riley's door. Helping her get unbuckled, I gripped her soft, rounded hips and lifted her out.

I turned back to Tuck and his step faltered when he spotted Riley beside me.

Riley's hand slid into mine and I had to hide my surprise, the pleasure of her seeking reassurance from me spreading warmth through my chest again. I curled my fingers around hers as Tuck reached us.

"Cash," he said before his gaze slid to Riley. "And who's this? You get me a present?"

Tucker's gaze was moving over Riley in a way I didn't like. Not at all. Tuck was handsome, joked around, smiled a lot, and had experience with women.

Once a year he paid for one to come from the city to stay with him for a month. To scratch that itch, he'd told me once. I flew them to him and back out again.

When his smile widened at Riley, I had to bite back the angry growl trying to crawl up my throat.

I caught and held his eyes. "Tucker, this is Riley. My wife."

Tuck's head jerked back, his eyes getting wide. "Wife?"

Riley stepped forward, and I tightened my hold on her hand as she held the other out for Tuck. He took it, and she graced him with one of her beautiful smiles.

"Nice to meet you, Tucker."

Jealousy gripped me, and I tugged her back, pulling her in close to me.

"Call me Tuck," he said, grinning. "How the hell did a big, ugly bastard like you find a beautiful woman like this?" Tucker asked me good-naturedly.

I wasn't feeling very good-natured myself, not when he turned that grin back on Riley. I ignored his question and opened the cargo door to start unloading his supplies, pulling Riley with me.

"We met online," she said.

"Never knew you had it in you," Tuck said to me.

I ignored him again.

"How long have you been married?"

"Not quite a week," Riley said.

Tuck chuckled. "Ah, so you'll be in the honeymoon phase? Can't keep your hands off each other, huh? Good thing I set up the mezzanine in the barn for you, Cash. You can be as noisy as you like out there and I won't hear a thing."

I did growl at that. "Not staying," I bit out. I had planned to, I always did. But I didn't want Riley around Tucker. I didn't like this feeling inside me. I didn't like the way he could talk and I couldn't. I didn't *want* him talking to her, and I didn't want him looking at her.

"Of course you are," Tuck said. "It's gonna be dark in another hour and I made supper. Got a nice bit of venison roasting."

I opened my mouth to tell him thanks but no, thanks, when Riley tugged on my hand. "Please, Cash. I don't think I could get back in that plane again today. And you must be tired?"

Her wide, pleading eyes cut off my refusal. We'd been flying all day, and she needed a break. I couldn't bear to do something to make her unhappy, so I gritted my teeth and nodded.

She released a relieved breath, squeezed my hand, and curled into my side. "Thank you."

Tuck clapped his hands. "Now that that's sorted, let's have a drink and some food."

I collected our bags and headed for the barn, and I kept Riley tucked against me the whole way.

---

RILEY THREW HER HEAD BACK, LAUGHING AT SOMETHING Tucker said. I couldn't look away, my heart thundering in my chest. My wife was beautiful. When she smiled, laughed, her whole face lit up. She'd had a little bit of Tucker's apple pie moonshine and her cheeks were flushed. Somehow that made her even more beautiful, when I didn't think that was possible.

Tuck would never touch her, I knew that, but there was no missing the way he was looking at her. He appreciated how lovely she was, was enjoying being in her company. I could only assume that Tuck was lonely like I'd been. He liked people, was good with them like Riley was, and I could tell they were both enjoying the chance to talk. It wasn't like I was much company for her.

"More?" Tuck said, holding up a mason jar of moonshine. "It's the Smith family secret recipe."

Riley's head tilted to the side. "You're a Smith?"

"Yup. Cash and I are cousins, though distant. Same with Beau and Hank. There are Smiths all over the area. We're obviously not a very adventurous bunch. We seem to put down roots and then hang in for the long haul."

"You don't get lonely?" Riley asked, her head tilting to the side.

Tucker's throat worked, but he grinned wide. "Nah, suits me this way." He took a sip of his drink. "So you two met online, huh?"

"We did."

Tucker glanced at me. "Guess that means you finally

caved, followed Beau's advice, and got satellite internet and a computer?"

I shook my head. "Just the internet, for Riley."

Riley frowned and turned to me. "You don't have a laptop?"

I shook my head.

"Then how did you email me?"

"Landon."

Riley frowned. "So you flew all the way to the general store to message me?"

I shook my head again. "He'd call. I'd tell him how to reply."

Her frown deepened. "Oh."

She didn't like that. My gut gripped tight.

"So what do you write?" Tucker asked, breaking the silence.

Riley turned back to Tucker. "Romance."

Every muscle in my body went rock solid. I hadn't even asked her that question. Why the hell hadn't I asked her what she wrote? And now I was sitting here in front of Tucker, looking like someone had just slapped my ass.

Tucker's brows rose. "Really?"

She nodded and took another sip of her drink before her gaze slid to me again. Her cheeks got pinker. "I love a happy ending."

"And how will that work now that you're living with Cash? Can you still make it work living out in the middle of nowhere?"

"It shouldn't be a problem." She glanced at me. "Like he said, Cash got me satellite internet. Hopefully, I can carry on without any hiccups."

Why hadn't I thought of that? Her writing and her readers were important to her, she'd told me that in one of her emails, and I hadn't even asked her what she needed or what I could do to help. I scowled, angry with myself, and angry that Tucker was the one asking her questions that I should have.

"So what kind of romance do you write?" Tuck asked.

"Erotic, mainly."

I choked on my drink.

"How interesting," Tuck said, his gaze sliding to me and grinning so wide I had to physically stop myself from strangling him.

*Erotic romance?*

"So you write about your couples being...intimate?" Tuck asked, eyes glittering, obviously enjoying himself.

"Yep, the bedroom door is wide open in my books. It's through sex and intimacy that their relationship grows and evolves."

I had no idea what any of that meant, but it was obvious my wife was far more experienced than me. Humiliation washed over me. How disappointed was she that she'd been stuck with me? She would have been better off with someone like Tucker, who asked her questions about her and her work, who made her laugh. A man who I could only assume, but didn't doubt, knew how to please a woman without instruction.

"I'd love to read some of your work sometime," Tuck said.

Riley beamed at him. "I'll make sure to bring you a few of my books next time we stay."

"I'd like that."

Riley was still grinning as she stood. "If you'll excuse me, gentlemen, I need the bathroom."

She left the room and Tucker turned to me, an expression on his face I'd never seen before.

"Jesus, Cash. Where the hell did you find her? You have to be the luckiest son of a bitch on this planet. Does she have a twin sister? Can we clone her? Shit, you done good, my friend."

"I know," I said, my voice hoarse, my gut in knots. "And she got stuck with me." Tuck and I were close. We talked, but I'd avoided topics that were too deep in the past.

Tuck frowned. "What the hell are you talking about? The way she looks at you? Honestly, I'm jealous as hell."

My next words came from my chest, my gut. The thing that I worried about most since I started talking to Riley. "What if I can't...make her happy."

Tucker's chin jerked back. "She already is."

He was wrong. He had no idea that I kept messing everything up. That I hadn't even known the kinds of books she wrote until right now, because *he'd* asked. How I'd had to get my wife to show me how to please her in bed.

And how I hadn't taken her properly yet, like I desperately wanted to, afraid that if I did, I'd hurt her because I was an animal who wanted to fuck his sweet, little wife so hard the bed would break.

Riley walked back in, and I cleared my throat, wanting her closer to me but not knowing how to ask for it.

"You want another drink, Riley?" Tuck asked.

"As delicious as your moonshine is, I better not or Cash will be carrying me to bed tonight," she said on a soft giggle.

My gut gripped tight, and then, like she could read my mind, instead of going back to her seat, she walked to me. I looked up at her as she took my hand, moving it out of my lap, and positioned herself between my spread knees. Her arm came around my neck, hand resting on my shoulder, and she perched her round, peachy behind on one of my thighs.

I stared at her in shock, my cock instantly hard, my heart racing a mile a minute, while the caveman in me roared with pleasure.

Her hand slid up the back of my neck, and she toyed with my hair, sending tingles all over my scalp. "Dinner was delicious, Tuck. Everything was perfect. I might have to get some tips from you. I'm not the best cook, and my husband has a big appetite."

I swallowed audibly at her calling me her husband, and as for my appetite, she had no idea. None. But it most certainly wasn't for food.

"Happy to," Tuck said, lips twitching.

There was humor in his voice, but I didn't look his way. I couldn't, not with Riley perched in my lap. Not when she pressed her thighs together like she had in the plane before we took off, like she was trying to soothe an ache.

"Right, well, I'm feeling a little tired," she said to Tucker. Her gaze came back to me, dipped to my lips. "I think I'm ready for bed, are you?"

Tuck chuckled low across from me, and I continued to ignore him.

"Yep," I said and stood, placing Riley on her feet.

"Night, Tucker," she said as I all but towed her from the room and out the door. I kept hold of her hand as we crossed the yard to the workshop.

This was where Tucker did his woodwork, and the smell of cedar and pine was strong when we walked in.

"Up here," I said to Riley, motioning to the stairs.

She walked up ahead of me, and I couldn't take my eyes off her lovely ass. A perfect peach. I wanted to lick all her juice, spread her wide, and slam inside.

I quickly adjusted my erection as we reached the top.

Riley stood there looking around the small space Tuck had set up for guests when he very occasionally had them.

"This is so cool," she said, taking everything in.

"There's an outhouse around the side of the barn if you need it later."

She screwed up her face. "An outhouse?"

She was cute when she did that, and I couldn't stop my chuckle. "Yep."

"Well, if I have to go out during the night, you're coming with me. I have no desire to be eaten by wolves while I'm peeing."

I chuckled again. I didn't do it often, but I liked it. And I liked the look on Riley's face when I did. I dipped my chin. I'd take her to the outhouse if she needed it, I'd take her anywhere she wanted to go.

I motioned to the bed. "Climb in. Get warm. I'll be back." I headed for the stairs to use the outhouse myself and grab a couple more blankets since it was cool tonight and I wanted Riley warm.

When I climbed back up a short time later, she had one of the lanterns by the bed going and was under the covers.

Her gaze dropped to the extra blankets. "Quick, get in, I need my husband to keep me warm."

My chest expanded from my sharply indrawn breath. I wanted her to call me that every day, all day. I'd never get enough of it. It made all this feel real. I wasn't on my own anymore. I had Riley. She was mine.

But I wasn't sure if she was ready for me to warm her the way I really wanted to tonight. Hell, every night since I'd picked her up at the general store close to a week ago.

I put one of the blankets on the chair by the bed and flicked out the other one, spreading it over her. She eyed me over the edge of the covers and didn't look away as I grabbed the back of my shirt and tugged it off over my head and tossed it onto the chair as well. No, her eyes dipped, gaze moving over my chest, down to my hands working my belt loose.

If she didn't look away now, she'd see how hard I was.

*She's had you in her hand, her mouth. There's nothing to be embarrassed about.* Still, my face warmed.

I expected her to avert her gaze, but as usual, my little wife surprised me and lifted to her elbows. To get a better view? My pulse thundered in my ears. I shoved my pants down, tossing them and my socks aside as well, leaving me in only my briefs.

My gaze slid over her—

*Oh God.*

Her shoulders were bare.

Was Riley naked under there?

Was I finally going to see her breasts? Was I finally going to get to touch them? Suck on her nipples? I'd seen them straining against her shirt, and not knowing what they looked like, how they felt against my lips, my tongue, had been driving me insane. I wanted it so bad.

*What if you lose control?*

I shook that thought loose. I wouldn't. How could I when all I wanted to do was take care of her? I'd keep control because *I had to*. The idea of hurting her made me sick to my stomach. Sex might not even be on the table tonight. I was okay with that, really I was. I was thankful for anything Riley gave me.

I'd happily bury my face between her thighs and stay there all night.

"Are you getting in?" she said softly. Her breathing had changed to shallow pants.

I'd been so caught up in the idea of seeing her naked, I hadn't noticed the way she was staring at my cock.

Lust washed over me so hard and fast I had no choice but to grab myself over my briefs and squeeze. Riley sat up and pulled the covers back. The sheet dropped away, revealing one full breast, pale and round, tipped with a mouthwatering rose-colored nipple.

"Riley," I choked out and stumbled toward her like a drunk man. Drunk on the sight of her. I climbed in, and the control I tried to call on dissolved into dust.

I shoved the covers away so I could see her, all of her. I *had* to.

She was half on her side, up on one elbow, and so incredibly beautiful, my throat tightened like a vise. Her breasts were large, full, enough to fill my hands. Her waist dipped in and her belly was rounded, the softness of it fuller below her belly button. God, I wanted to nuzzle it. My gaze traveled over her hips flaring out and along her smooth thighs.

My mouth watered, and I moved closer, unable to stop myself. Riley dropped back, looking up at me as I dipped my face to her throat, running my nose, my lips down over her collarbone.

"So beautiful, darlin'," I said, voice guttural.

Her hand drifted over my shoulder. "So are you, Cash. You have no idea, do you?"

I dragged in a rough breath at her words. Then watched her, judging her reaction as I finally took her breasts in my hands, testing their weight. *Sweet Jesus.* There was no stopping me from sucking a nipple into my mouth. I nearly cried from the pleasure of it.

She moaned, her fingers drifting over my neck, my head, threading through my hair.

"I—I think we've waited long enough, don't you, Cash?"

My arms closed around her all on their own as I struggled to breathe. My cock throbbed, the hot, heavy weight of it, the deep ache in my lower gut and balls almost unbearable. "You're gonna let me have you?" There was no holding back any of it—the words came tumbling out of my mouth. "Oh, Christ. Oh, please, Riley, being with you like that, pushing deep inside you...I don't think I'll survive it. But, darlin'...I'll die if you say no."

Her legs moved restlessly beneath mine. "Do you have any idea what you do to me when you say things like that? It's me that won't survive you."

Breathing hard, I took her hand from my neck and rubbed my thumb over the rings she wore, the ones that told the world she was mine. I brought her hand to my lips and kissed her precious fingers.

I didn't deserve her, this.

But I was going to take what she offered. Take everything she was willing to give.

And I was going to keep her, no matter what.

## 7

## RILEY

CASH LOOMED OVER ME, eyes wild. His chest was pumping, and his breath huffed in and out.

"Are you sure, Riley?" he asked, his voice like gravel.

I nodded and cupped his cheek. His color was high and his beard tickled my palm. I wanted him, and there was no use pretending otherwise. "You're driving me crazy, Cash Smith. I don't think I can wait another second, let alone another day. I know we're still getting to know each other, but I feel...a connection to you. I want this. I want you."

His gaze went from wild to blazing hot. He liked that I wanted him. And I realized he hadn't had a lot of that in his life. How could he when he'd been on his own so long?

"I can't think anymore now that you're with me," he growled. "I can't work and I can't sleep from wanting you so bad."

I slid my hand over his shoulder, down his chest dusted with dark hair, and over the thick slabs of his abs. He was so incredibly strong. I loved everything about his body. "I'm yours. Your wife. You don't have to want anymore, Cash," I whispered and ran my thumb over his lower lip. "You can have."

His entire body jolted hard enough that the bed shook. "I can?"

"Yes," I whispered.

He made a desperate sound and lowered his head again, sucking a nipple into his mouth. One hand covered the opposite breast and massaged restlessly, almost roughly, while the other slid down to my butt and grabbed on. He sucked and licked and toyed with my nipples until I couldn't take it, until my thighs were slick and I was squirming with how much I wanted him.

And all the while his hands, those massive, rough hands moved over my body, squeezing and massaging. My skin would be pink from it, marked from his calloused palms. It felt fantastic. I could feel where he'd been as well as where he was, and the overload of sensation was more than I could take.

His mouth moved to my other nipple, and I cried out. "Please. Please, Cash, I need you."

The hand at my waist slid back down to my bottom, squeezed, then moved between my thighs. He hissed. "So wet. Christ, you want me? Don't you, darlin'?" he choked out as if the idea amazed him.

At those growled-out words, sweet and dirty at the same time, I spread my thighs wider and rolled my hips, trying to get him to give me his fingers while he continued to play with my tormented nipple. "Y-yes, I want you."

He cursed and pressed two fingers against my opening, then slowly pushed the tips inside. "How badly does my little wife want her husband's cock?" he said so deep, I felt it low in my belly. "Who do you need, Riley? Say it for me, I need to hear it again."

My thighs started to shake. "My husband. I need my husband inside me."

He slid deeper, and I moaned from the pleasure of it, from the sweet invasion of his thick fingers.

He made that same desperate sound, staring into my eyes. "You're so tight. Oh God, you're so tight, darlin'. So small. I don't wanna hurt you."

My back arched as he dragged his fingers out and thrust back in. "Y-you won't, I promise."

His massive body trembled almost violently. "The way I want you, Riley..." His eyes slid away from mine. "I know I'll hurt you."

He looked tormented.

I sat up, and his fingers slid from me. I bit back my moan, ignored his worried expression, and pushed at his shoulder. He dropped to his back, and pain transformed his features. He thought I was going to stop. That I was rejecting him. It was in his eyes.

I quickly straddled his hips, not wanting to see that look on his face another second. "It's okay," I whispered and leaned down, pressing my mouth to his. His arms came up instantly, locking around me, like he truly thought I would leave. I kissed him some more, then said against his lips, "I'm going to ride you this first time. Then I have control over how much of you I take and how fast we go, okay?"

His arms spasmed around me, his breath sawing in and out. He didn't answer, just gritted his teeth. Cash was trying desperately to hold himself back. I'd teach him that he didn't have to. That I wouldn't break. That whatever he wanted was okay. That between us it would be amazing.

I moved back, sitting on his thighs. His cock was thick and long and swollen in front of me, standing straight up against his stomach, pre-come leaking from the head. He had to be in serious pain. I slid over it so my pussy pressed against the underside of his length and rocked, rolling my hips, sliding up and back, coating him in me.

Cash hissed out a breath, his hands clamping onto my hips and yanking me down so I was grinding harder against his cock trapped between our bodies.

That's when I realized I didn't have a condom. We hadn't talked about contraception. So stupid of me.

"Cash," I said, and his eyes that were locked between my thighs, shot up to mine. "I'm clean, I've been tested, and I've never had sex without a condom. I'm also on the pill," I said.

Cash's eyes flashed.

He didn't like talking about the men I'd been with in the past, so I quickly carried on. "What I'm trying to say is, are you okay with us not using a condom?"

"Yes," he gritted out and lifted his hips, still holding mine and grinding against me harder this time.

I gasped and rolled my hips, sliding back enough that I could take his cock in my hand and angle it up. I pumped it a couple of times, then notched the head at my opening.

Cash growled as I planted my free hand against his shoulder and lowered myself so the head slipped inside. His entire body went still, every muscle going rock solid. I bit my lip, my gaze sliding back to his, and what I saw there made me quiver, made me want him even more. Made me hunger for the dark secrets he was afraid to share, the things he wanted to do to me.

I sat back, taking more, and gasped.

"*Oh fuck*, that's it. That's it. Work me inside you, darlin'." More hissed breaths. "You can take me, can't you, sweetheart? You can take all of me?"

His words were half order, half desperate hope.

I lifted up a bit, then came back down, taking more of him. He cursed roughly, and his fingers dug deeper into my hips, flexing and releasing. My mouth dropped open on a cry as I took more, as he stretched me wide. He filled me like nothing I'd ever experienced before.

"Yes," I said and licked my lip. "Yes, I can take all of you."

"Then do it, Riley. Sink all the way down. Please, *oh Christ*, do it."

Again, there was that mix of a demand and desperation. It was intoxicating. I kept my eyes locked with his as I gave him what he demanded from me. I tried to relax my inner muscles and sat back, letting his incredibly thick, long cock slide in deep, until I had every hot, hard, relentless inch of him.

I made an incoherent sound as a deep tremor moved through me, out of me, until my limbs trembled and my breath shook.

Cash clenched his teeth, and I pressed both hands against his shoulders, moving them over his chest restlessly. I rolled my hips and gasped. His hands slid from my hips to my waist and back, encouraging me without words to move.

I started slow, allowing myself to adjust to his size, to the sweet ache he gave me.

My legs were stretched wide, and with the way he filled me, every time I came down on him, the base of his cock grazed my clit. It was too much, too good.

Cash gripped my waist harder, and on an urgent cry, he slammed up, like he couldn't stop himself from moving any longer.

I cried out, nearly coming.

"You love it, don't you, wife? You love how full I make you feel?"

I never expected my quiet, sometimes awkward husband to let loose when we were in bed. But he did. He couldn't hold back what he was thinking, what he wanted. I wanted more of it. I wanted him to give me everything. "Yes. Yes, I love it."

His hand went to where we were joined, feeling himself slide in and out of my body, then his thumb slid over my clit. "This was made for me, Riley. You were meant to answer my ad, weren't you, darlin'? You were always meant to be mine?"

"Yes," I said and moved faster, coming down harder, his thickness stretching me, making me burn in the best way, hitting just right deep inside, over and over. He worked my clit faster, and my head fell back. "Oh God, I'm going to—" I cried out, calling Cash's name as I shook and shuddered and clamped down tight on his huge cock buried inside me.

I fell against his chest, gasping, panting, trembling as my orgasm washed through me—

Cash made a sound that lifted goose bumps all over my skin, and a second later I was flipped to my back. He covered my body with his and slammed inside me. One hand came around the back of my neck, gripping it, the other was planted in the mattress by my waist. He thrust into me again with enough force to slam the headboard into the wall.

He dragged his mouth over mine—not really a kiss, just lips touching—then stared down at me, his face taut with pleasure. "*Oh fuck. Oh fuck.*"

My eyes rolled back when his huge body drove into me again. I wrapped my arms around his shoulders, clinging to him as he started fucking me hard enough to make the ground shake.

He continued to stare down at me, a wildness in his eyes. "I don't want to hurt you...I don't..." He pounded deep again, like his body wasn't his own.

I cupped his face. "D-don't stop. You're not hurting me." I moaned low. "God, Cash, I'm close to coming again. Fuck me like you need to. Fuck me like you've been wanting to."

He made a broken, gasping sound and let loose. I thought he was pounding into me hard before. Now, I was surprised the bed didn't go through the wall. It was…incredible.

I'd feel it for days. I'd feel *him* for days. I wanted to.

"Cash!" A scream was torn from me as another orgasm rolled through me. I hung on to him, my body jolting as he continued to thrust deep. My inner muscles were clamping down on his thick, unforgiving length, so tight, I couldn't catch my breath. Lost in the pleasure of finally being taken the way I'd needed to be for so long. The way only Cash could.

He released my neck and lifted to his arms, his back bowing, rocking his hips into me with force. He roared as he came, pulsing deep inside me, pumping me full.

He claimed me in that moment. Cash had made me his, and now there was no going back.

I was fine with that. I didn't want to be anywhere else.

I'd claimed him, too.

---

*CASH*

I glanced at Riley again and had to bite back a possessive growl. When we'd taken off this morning, heading for my cousin's house, she'd grabbed my arm like she always did, but she didn't close her eyes, she kept her gaze on me.

Like I was somehow capable of taking her fears away.

God, she was so incredibly beautiful. Her hair was down

and wavy, a little wild, her color high, eyes bright. My wife was glowing, and I hoped it had something to do with what we did last night, because I would *never* be the same. I was altered. She had altered me.

An image of Riley straddling my hips, taking me inside her over and over again was embedded in my brain, was all I could think about—

She shifted in her seat and winced.

My body went rock solid. "Riley?"

A smile lit up her gorgeous face. "Hmm?"

"You're in pain."

Her cheeks darkened. "I'm fine, Cash."

I'd hurt her.

I'd fucking hurt my precious, little wife with my big, clumsy hands and my giant, oversized body. With the way I'd taken her last night.

I was going to be sick.

Here I was thinking how life-changing last night had been, and Riley was sitting beside me in pain because I'd fucked her like a barbarian.

"You're not," I bit out and had to swallow several times when acid crawled up my throat. "I hurt you."

She reached out, her fingers curling around my forearm. "No...Cash, look at me."

I did as she asked, looking into her pretty brown eyes.

"I'm a little sore..."

I groaned, sucking in a ragged breath, and had to look away as my stomach rebelled.

"Cash," Riley said more forcefully. "Look at me."

I forced myself to turn back to her as she leaned closer, as much as she could while strapped into her seat.

"I'm a little sore because I haven't had sex in a long time.

I have a husband who is big…everywhere, and you fucked me hard."

My fingers gripped the control wheel tighter, and I shook my head. I couldn't even bear to hear it. "I'm sorry," I choked out. "I won't…I won't ever do that again. I won't…"

"I loved it, Cash. *Loved it*. I love the way you took me hard, and I loved the way you let go of that control of yours."

My gaze sliced back to her. "What?"

"And I love that I can still feel you inside me, even now. Every time I move I'm reminded of the way you took me."

"You liked that?" I rasped.

"My nipples are still tender from the way you sucked them, and my skin is oversensitive from the way your beard and those wide, rough-skinned hands of yours moved over my body. No one has ever made me feel the way you did. No one has ever taken me the way you did. And every time I move, I get hotter, more desperate for my husband to ease the ache that's been building again since I woke this morning."

My cock was hard in an instant. "I thought…"

"I know what you thought, Cash. But what you need to *know* is what you gave me last night is exactly what I've been craving for so long. You said while you were moving inside me that we were made for each other. I think you might be right about that because I've never experienced anything so wonderful in my life."

I sat there stunned silent, trying to focus on her words while all the blood in my brain drained to my cock. "You liked it?" I said again, like a damned idiot.

She giggled, free and sweet, her face flushed, and I almost came.

A smile curled her lips. "Hurry up and get us somewhere that you can kiss it and make it better, already."

I dragged in a sharp breath. "I'm gonna need you to stop talking now."

She batted her lashes at me. "Hey, what did I do?"

Now all I could think about was her pussy under my tongue. "You know what you did."

Her gaze dipped to my hard-on, and I growled.

She bit her lips together, trying not to smile. "Okay, change of subject? Would that help?"

I grunted, but inside I was so happy, I was close to pounding my chest and roaring with pleasure.

"Favorite color?" she asked.

I frowned.

"Stop with the frowning and answer my questions."

Now I had to bite back a smile. "Green."

"Mine's red. Favorite food?"

"Meat."

She giggled again, and I cursed. The woman had not a clue, none, what that did to me.

"No giggling," I said, even as my gaze slid to her lovely rosebud mouth.

"I don't giggle."

"You do. Sounds like little bells."

She blinked over at me, all wide-eyed and so pretty my dick got harder. "Really? And that's a bad thing?"

"Makes me hard." There was no point pretending otherwise.

"As far as I can tell, you're always hard."

"Yep."

She giggled again.

"Riley," I gritted out.

She giggled harder.

"Not helping, woman."

"Okay, sorry. Where were we? That's right...*meat*." She

made a little snorting sound, fighting another fit of giggles. Not only did that make my dick throb, it was cute as hell. "My favorite food is vegetarian lasagna."

"Sounds disgusting."

She cried in outrage, and I bit back another grin.

"It's delicious. I'll make it for you."

I grunted.

"Now you're just being rude."

"Didn't say anything, wife."

"You grunt a lot...that was your 'your cooking sucks, Riley' grunt."

"Nope."

She twisted more in her seat. "Okay, what was it, then?"

"My 'you can make it, but I ain't eatin' it' grunt."

Her eyes narrowed. "Oh, you'll eat it."

I groaned. "Don't talk about eating things, either."

She bit her lips together again, but they were curling up at the sides. "We've circled back, haven't we?"

I growled a warning.

"You know, to the 'kissing it and making it better' part of the conversation?"

"Didn't need you to spell it out."

"I know." Now she wasn't even trying to hide her grin.

I shook my head. In pain. Frustrated as hell. And happier than I'd ever been in my life.

I couldn't wait to get her somewhere so I could have her again.

"Wow, you look kind of grumpy," she said, sounding far too happy about it.

I growled again, and she laughed.

It was even better than her giggle.

I still had another thirty minutes trapped in here with my sexy wife until we reached Beau's place. With her scent filling the cockpit, driving me to distraction. With her laughter ringing in my ears, and her sweet smiles constantly aimed my way.

I wasn't sure I'd survive it.

But at least I'd die happy.

8
___

# RILEY

Sunday night was family dinner night for the Smiths. Apparently, they alternated between Hank's and Beau's houses, since they lived close, and this week Beau and Freya were hosting.

I sat at the huge dinner table, crowded with Cash's family. Cash on one side, three-year-old Conner on the other, and one-year-old Charlotte on my lap.

Given that I had never experienced anything like this in my life, I was feeling more than a little overwhelmed.

Hank and Beau were huge like their cousin. Their wives, Birdie and Freya, who had welcomed me with open arms, had loaded the table with enough food for an army, which wasn't far from the truth since Hank and Birdie had twins, *two sets*—Emmy and Beth, aged six, and Jake and Oliver, aged two. And Beau and Freya had Conner, Five, *and yes,* one-year-old twins as well—Charlotte and Baxter.

Charlotte was squirming like crazy in my lap, and I looked around, unsure what to do. I glanced at Cash, who was holding her twin. Baxter was fast asleep. Everyone was eating—or trying to, in my case—while they chatted and passed plates of food.

Hank and Beau sat to Cash's left at one end of the table, and the three men were talking, though that was probably a stretch. Beau talked and Hank and Cash did a lot of grunting. Obviously, a family trait. The kids didn't stay in their seats; they shifted around, constantly climbing on and off laps—and no one seemed bothered by all the moving about. Soon, the food that I thought we'd never get through was almost gone.

So yes, overwhelmed was an understatement.

"Let me take that little monster," Beau said, standing and lifting his daughter from my lap. "You need to eat." He turned and looked at his wife. "Can you get me a beer, Bear?"

*Bear?*

She flipped him off but handed him one. "Prepare for payback," she said and smiled sweetly, but there was no missing the promise of revenge.

Cash turned to me and frowned down at my plate. Why didn't that surprise me? He was always worried about me eating enough, even though I certainly didn't look like I was starving.

I smiled at Beau. "Your daughter is adorable."

"She also never sleeps."

"Try having four that don't sleep," Hank said, as Jake and Oliver climbed their father like little spider monkeys. Hank steadied them while they stood on his solid thighs, one with his arms wrapped around Hank's neck, the other trying to hang off the arm supporting him.

Hank made a growling sound and stood suddenly. The boys squealed, giggling with delight as he carried them to the living room. He ended up on the floor, his boys climbing all over him laughing hysterically. The other kids piled in, and soon Beau joined in, a pile of giant men and giggling children.

I could see now why Cash wanted kids of his own. He didn't say much, but there was no missing how much he loved his family.

"Okay?" he asked.

I nodded. "I mean, it's a lot to take in. This only child spent most of her time alone. But this is nice and...noisy."

"Yep," he said, his gaze softening as he chuckled. "Eat, Riley. You haven't had much all day."

I filled my fork with roast meat and potatoes. "Do you come here a lot?"

Cash stared pointedly at my fork, waiting for me to put it in my mouth. Only when I was chewing did he answer.

"Usually once a month."

I nodded, chewing. "And this is all the family you have left, right? I mean, besides all your distant cousins scattered all over the place?"

He nodded but frowned, head tilting to the side, looking confused.

"You told me in one of your emails," I reminded him and scooped up more mashed potato.

"I did?"

"You did. So you guys are pretty close? I like seeing this side of you."

"Come on, Uncle Cash," Emmy said, grabbing his hand.

He turned to her and smiled, and it was so full of warmth and love, it stole my breath. He let her pull him out of his seat, and he joined the wrestling match on the living room floor. I couldn't contain my laughter.

"Here, let me top off your glass," Freya said, sitting down beside me.

"Thanks."

Birdie walked over as well and sat down. "With any luck, they'll wear my brood out and I'll get a few hours' sleep tonight."

Freya shook her head. "Either that or they'll be so overexcited they won't sleep at all."

Birdie groaned.

Cash's deep, rumbling laugh reached me, and I turned to see him "fighting off" Jake and Oliver.

"He's so good with them," Freya said, a soft smile curling her lips. "They love when he visits."

"So how are things going?" Birdie asked. "Cash isn't the most, um...talkative guy. I guess he's similar to Hank in that way. It can be...frustrating."

"Ah, yes. Let's just say I've been working hard on my mind-reading skills, and I'm not sure how accurate they are."

Cash glanced at me, his eyes locking on mine for a moment. Memories of the night before flashed through my mind, and I pulled in a sharp breath.

"But then, who needs to talk?" Freya said and laughed softly.

She hadn't missed my new husband's heated look, but then it wasn't very subtle. I tried to fight my grin and failed. "There are definitely other aspects of our relationship that are progressing...very well."

Freya took a sip of her wine. "With these guys, that's how they show affection, how they communicate their feelings."

Birdie nodded sagely. "Being physical comes naturally to them. They use their bodies, their hands, all day. They've been isolated, Hank and Cash especially, their whole lives. A verbal response comes second to a physical one more often than not. I learned quickly that Hank needs a lot of physical contact from me, even if it is just a hug. I mean, we're an old married couple now, but in the beginning, it was a language he understood and stopped him from feeling...insecure or unsure, I guess."

That made sense, and it definitely helped confirm my experience. I'd never met a man like Cash, and I felt out of my depth more often than not. "When we emailed each other, he was a lot more open. It's been hard to merge that Cash with this one, but I think we're getting there slowly."

Freya rested her hand on mine. "It was hard at the beginning for Beau and me, too, and he's the chatty one. Then again, *some* of that might have been my fault, just a tiny bit."

Birdie giggled.

Freya scowled at her sister-in-law, then rolled her eyes. "You may as well know, since you're one of us now, and they love to tease me relentlessly about it. When I met Beau online, I pretended I knew more than I did about living in a place like this. But in my defense, I took one look at his picture and fell instantly in love with him. Then and there, I decided to make myself into the woman he'd advertised for...by watching Bear Grylls in action on the Discovery Channel." She narrowed her eyes at her husband. "Yes, I know. I was an idiot. He figured it out pretty quick, and yes, things were a little rocky for us at the beginning, but we worked it out. Now I can fish like a pro, but Beau still loves to tease me, hence the nickname 'Bear.'"

Birdie cracked up, and I did as well. Then we kept on laughing as Freya regaled us with tales of her exploits pretending she was an outdoors woman, while Beau let her squirm.

When the laughing died down, I glanced back at Cash. He was watching me, warmth in his eyes, and I gave him a knowing smile.

"It won't be easy," Birdie said, drawing my attention back to her. "I didn't find Hank the same way you and Freya met Beau and Cash, but I know what it's like to try to connect with these guys. I felt insecure a lot because I had no idea what Hank was thinking. I had to change my mindset. You can't compare these guys with any other man you've been with. They don't play games. What you see is what you get."

"That's...reassuring, but also a little frightening," I said.

"Yeah, it can be, and hard to get used to. And probably even more so with a man like Cash, since he's been on his own so long," Freya said.

I sipped my drink, quietly observing my husband with his family. I had assumed he just needed time, that eventually he'd relax with me, talk more. Now I wasn't so sure that would happen. "Maybe we should start writing to each other again," I said, chuckling as I thought about his beautiful emails, even as my heart tightened a little bit.

Finding out Landon had been the go-between had definitely come as a shock. He knew everything we'd said to each other. Some of it very personal. But I guess I couldn't be angry. Without Landon's help, I wouldn't be here now.

"If you ever need to talk, we're here," Birdie said.

Freya filled my glass again. "Absolutely. Anything you need, we're here for you. You're family now, and I for one am happy you are."

---

CASH

Riley's soft footfalls reached me as she came down the stairs.

The house was silent; the others had gone to bed. Riley had just finished in the bathroom, and I turned to watch as she rounded the corner. She was wearing a long-sleeve thermal top and tiny sleep shorts. Light from the fire danced over her curves, making her skin glow.

I wanted to strip her down and have her naked.

"Okay?" I asked, throat tight with need. Being around a big family like this wasn't something she was used to.

She smiled. "Better than okay."

I moved toward her with purpose and scooped her up. She giggled softly as I carried her across the room and laid her on our makeshift bed on Beau and Freya's living room floor.

I covered her, staying up on my elbow so she didn't take my weight. "You still hurting, darlin'?" I asked. Despite her reassurances, I still worried that I'd caused her pain. It was all I'd been able to think about.

She slid her hands over my shoulders, one curving around the side of my neck, the other brushing over my beard. "I'm fine, I promise."

I shifted, bringing my hands in between us and covered her breasts, massaging their heavy weight. She moaned softly, and I stared into her brown eyes, making sure there was only pleasure, no pain.

"I like your family," she murmured.

Yeah, I'd gotten that. It'd been hard to miss. This made me happier than I knew what to do with.

"I'm glad you have them," she whispered.

"Me too."

"I usually spent the holidays alone at boarding school or with my grandmother. I think my folks had me, then realized the whole parenting thing wasn't for them." She shook her head. "What I'm trying to say is, I've never experienced anything like I did tonight. I really liked it, Cash. And I like them a lot."

Christ, she tore my heart right out of my chest. How could someone leave Riley behind? How could they not want to be with her every second of every day?

"They really like you, too, darlin'."

I stopped massaging and slid her top up slowly, revealing her lovely, soft, bare breasts. My breathing turned shaky as I cupped the sides, lifting them, pressing them together, then leaning in and gently sucking one of her nipples into my mouth.

We both moaned. I kept it gentle, not something I was good at, but she needed that from me after last night, after the way I'd taken her.

I sucked, soft and light, one nipple and then the other, until she was squirming and restless beneath me. "Gonna take care of you," I rasped, meaning it in every way that it could, and kissed my way down her rounded belly, skin smooth, breathing in her delicate scent.

A scent that was now branded on my senses for the rest of my life.

My mouth traveled along the edge of her shorts. "You still need me to kiss it better, wife?"

"Yes. Yes, I do," she said, fingers sliding through my hair.

I gripped the elastic waistband of her shorts and tugged them and her panties all the way down her legs, then tossed them aside. I spread her wide and took in her slick, swollen pussy, licking my lips, my mouth now watering for her.

Leaning in, I gently lapped her up. She was hot and so wet. Perfect. I settled in, getting comfortable. I wanted to make her feel good, that's all I needed. Yes, I wanted back inside her, but I'd die before I'd hurt her. If she needed time after last night, I'd give it to her. I'd give her anything.

I licked and sucked her carefully, slowly kissing her pussy until she was panting and her fingers were fisting my hair tight. I didn't stop or change pace, just kept things slow and soft, ignoring the driving need of my cock and focusing solely on Riley and making her feel good.

She was panting now, her thighs spreading wider before closing and pressing against the side of my head as she rolled her hips. I wrapped my arms around her silky thighs, holding them there, licking from her opening to her clit, sucking lightly before sliding back down. Over and over, I licked and sucked, then finally, I dipped my tongue inside her before moving back up to her clit and suckling a bit longer.

I repeated the move, pressing my tongue a little deeper, sucking her clit a little longer with every pass, until Riley was quivering, her breasts shaking, her hips squirming.

"I need you," she said. "I want you inside me when I come, Cash."

I stilled. "You sure?"

She whimpered. "Yes."

I rose up over her, and her hands dropped to my briefs, shoving them down as she wrapped her legs around my waist. Her hands found my cock, and she led me exactly where she wanted me. I squeezed my eyes closed as the head slipped inside.

*Oh hell.*

She wasn't ready for this. How could she be after the way I fucked her the night before? But as I looked down at her, my hips angled forward like they had a mind of their own, and I slid deeper. There was no pain on her face, just pleasure.

"Yes, Cash, more." She tugged me down, and I kissed her hard, groaning against her lips as she flicked her tongue inside, tasting me, tasting herself.

I started to move, keeping things slow, easy, not wanting

to hurt her again. Riley tore her mouth from mine, arching against me, and her fingers dug into my ass as she ground up against me.

"Darlin'," I bit out. "Trying to be careful with you."

Riley was lost to her pleasure, and it was the most beautiful thing I'd ever seen. Her eyes were glassy and heavy, her lips puffy, mouth open. "Harder, Cash," she said and gasped. "Please, I need you to fuck me harder."

My control was hanging by a thread. "Riley...Jesus."

"I want it," she said, then moaned helplessly.

I could deny her nothing. And the hot, unrelenting need to thrust deep and hard won out at her plea. I withdrew, then snapped my hips forward, slamming into her.

She arched under me, crying out. "Yes. Again."

I quickly covered her mouth with my hand, and her eyes glazed over, the pleasure on her face unmistakable. She was going to kill me. My sweet, sexy, little wife was going to destroy me with every thrust of my hips, with every clutch of her tight-as-hell pussy.

"Gonna take my hand away. Can you be quiet?" I rasped.

She shook her head and one of her hands left my ass, covering my hand over her mouth, asking me without words to keep it there.

*Oh, Christ in Heaven.*

My hips slammed against hers again—instinct, hunger, need taking over, driving my cock in deep, almost brutally. Her hand flew back to my ass, digging her nails in.

I locked eyes with hers, getting lost in her hunger for me, feeding off it, and started fucking her like she wanted me to, like I desperately needed to be.

Slow. Hard. Deep.

Her body jarred with each of my thrusts, her gaze getting hotter, her hold on me tighter. I couldn't look away. I was addicted to the sight of her getting off on the way I fucked her. How much she loved me stuffing her full of me. How much she loved her big, clumsy, inexperienced husband pounding into her like a wild, rutting bull.

My fingers were still curled tight over her mouth. And on the next brutal thrust, she tightened around me. Her eyes widened. She was close. I picked up the pace, slamming into her harder, faster. "Gonna come," I growled out. "You gonna come with me, wife?"

She nodded.

I pounded into the perfect, tight heat of her body, twice more, and she arched beneath me, her nails clawing at my skin, her inner muscles gripping me so tight I saw stars. I didn't let up. I thrust into her over and over as her muffled cries washed over me, as my balls drew up, cock pulsing, and I shot hot and hard, deep inside her. *Oh God*. Her pussy pulsed around me relentlessly, taking everything I had.

I was still deep inside her when she went pliant, when her muffled cries stopped and her grip loosened. I took my hand away and kissed her swollen lips. Riley curled her arms around my neck, and I wrapped her in mine, rolling to my side, taking her with me.

We stayed like that for a long time, kissing, stroking, holding each other.

I didn't know how it happened so fast, but I was in so deep with Riley that I hated even letting her go to the bathroom without me. Had to stop myself from trailing her up the stairs just so I could keep my arms around her and my mouth on hers.

This could only mean one thing, and it terrified the hell out of me. It was too soon. I could still lose her. But there was no mistaking it.

I'd fallen in love with my sweet, little wife.

# 9

## RILEY

I WOKE AND STRETCHED, yawning wide, then opened my eyes.

Cash was standing by our bed, a mug of hot chocolate in his hand and an odd look on his face.

I blinked up at him. "Good morning."

He'd kept me up late. It had been like that the last two weeks. My husband was insatiable. Not that I minded in the least, but unlike him, I found it harder to spring out of bed in the morning. Often by the time I woke, he'd been out working on the property or in the workshop for several hours.

He handed me my hot chocolate, and I took a sip, letting the caffeine do its thing.

"You had a bad dream last night," he said, eyes boring into mine.

I froze. "Did I?"

He made a rumbly sound. "You've had a few."

I'd been so sure he'd slept through them. God, I wasn't ready to talk about it with Cash. I didn't want to ruin the present by bringing up the past, not now when we were still finding our feet as a couple. "Huh, weird," I said, probably unconvincingly.

He watched me for several long seconds more, and I smiled up at him and took another sip of my drink. He frowned, but then his wide shoulders relaxed.

"Come on," he finally said, thankfully dropping the topic. "Wanna show you something."

I did as he asked. I was in pj shorts that I'd tugged on after Cash had made me come three times and a tank. It was cool, so I slipped on the long, sloppy cardigan I'd been using like a robe and shoved my feet in my Ugg boots and took his hand.

He let me.

He always let me. Cash never initiated the hand holding, but he didn't seem to mind when I laced my fingers with his. I thought—hoped—he liked it as much as me.

Cash led me down the hall to the door that led to the new extension at the back of the house. He opened it, and we walked in. We had walls, a roof, and he'd laid the floorboards in the last few weeks. There was still a lot to do before it would be useable, but it was already pretty awesome.

He led me to the door on the left. It was my favorite room. It had a spectacular view of the mountains, but I could also see Cash's barn/workshop out the window.

The door swung open, and I froze at the threshold.

While we'd spent every night together, we had our own things to do during the day. Cash did what Cash did, and I wrote. I had a deadline to meet, and I'd been hiding away in the bedroom, working on my book, then usually I'd make dinner. Sometimes Cash would.

Which was why I'd had no idea that he'd been working on this room.

I twisted to look at him, and he was watching me, his color high, hands moving restlessly at his sides.

"How did you find the time to do all this?" I whispered.

The floor was polished, the walls painted a beautiful duck-egg blue. There was a huge bookshelf against one wall and a desk...the most exquisite desk I'd ever seen, sitting in the middle of the room. My laptop was on it, along with all my notebooks and journals.

"Will it do?" he asked.

I opened my mouth, closed it, trying to find the right words.

He shoved his fingers through his hair. "You get a sore back sitting on the bed or at the kitchen table. Can tell in the evenings."

I nodded.

"So..." He motioned to the desk again.

"You made it?"

He nodded.

"And the bookshelf?"

He nodded again.

"For me?"

Another nod.

"You did all of this...for me?"

He didn't nod this time, he just stared at me.

"Cash, it's...it's beautiful. All of it." I put my mug on top of one of my notebooks, turned, and flew at him. He caught me instantly, and I hugged him tight, peppering his face with kisses. "I love it. I love it so much."

His deep chuckles vibrated against my chest, and I loved that, too. He carried me to the desk and set my butt on the varnished top.

"Glad," he said gruffly.

There was an old, worn leather chair behind it. It looked

well loved. "Where did you find the chair?" I ran my fingers over the buttery soft leather.

"It was my mom's."

His expression was carefully blank. Always keeping his feelings locked away. The only time I got more out of him was when we were naked. It bothered me. I'd been here for three weeks now. No, that wasn't *that* long, but I assumed after he felt more comfortable around me, he'd start to share, even just a little.

I rested my hand on his chest. "Thank you, I'm honored you'd let me use it."

"It's yours," he said just as gruffly.

He stood back and let me climb down and try it out. Oh yes, it was incredibly comfortable and the perfect height for the desk.

I flipped my laptop open.

He moved my drink closer to me, and I quickly grabbed the notebook and put it under it. No way did I want mug rings on my gorgeous desk. I smiled up at him.

His amazing blue eyes scanned my face. "I've got some work to do."

"Okay," I said. I didn't want him to go, but instead of saying that, I said, "No one's ever done anything like this for me. Not ever."

My parents had occasionally sent me gifts from their travels, but they didn't know me, had never known me. There'd been no love, no meaning behind the things they sent. Just a way to assuage their guilt.

His nostrils flared and his chest expanded, then he dipped his chin and walked out.

I took in my beautiful new office and blinked rapidly. So much thought had gone into every detail.

I looked back to my laptop, opened my work in progress,

and started to write. When I was in the city, I'd struggled. Stress and fear had made it impossible to get the words down. But here, with Cash, they were flowing.

———

I GLANCED UP FROM MY WORK AND DID A DOUBLE TAKE AT THE time. I'd been at it for three hours. There was a muffin and a cup of tea beside me, and the heater had been turned on in the corner of the room. I'd been so in the zone, I hadn't even noticed Cash walk in. I glanced out the window. He was walking across the field, back to his workshop.

I took a bite out of my muffin. I'd made them yesterday. They weren't half bad. I was no culinary goddess, but at least I was improving. While I sipped my drink, I filed away my notebooks in the bottom drawer, grinning to myself when I found the emails Cash and I had exchanged, the ones I'd printed off. I'd planned to scrapbook them before I came, a memento for us both, but hadn't gotten around to it.

I put them in the drawer as well.

After a bathroom break, I got back to work, reading over the last few paragraphs I'd written. I'd finish this draft by the end of the week at this rate.

A repetitive sound had me lifting my head a while later. I glanced at the time. *3 p.m.* Another three hours had ticked by. I'd been sitting here in my fabulous, new office nearly all day. And I'd been so engrossed in my work, I still hadn't gotten out of my pj's.

The plate that had my muffin on it was empty, so was the tea. So I'd obviously finished them during my writing frenzy. The repetitive sound, loud and jarring, came again and had me looking out the window. The chair squeaked in the silent room, and I kind of froze, my mouth dropping open at the sight before me.

Cash was outside the barn. His shirt was off, and he was wielding an ax like a marauding Viking. His expression was harsh, focused, as he brought the ax down on an innocent chunk of wood, cleaving it in two with one brutal *whack*. His bare chest glistened with sweat despite the cooler temperature. He scooped the chunks of wood off the ground and tossed them onto a pile against the barn wall, and the thick slabs of muscles in his arms, chest, and stomach danced in a way that made my mouth water.

Cash had a warrior's body, his muscles built from years of hard physical labor—thick and heavy, wrapped around his large, solid frame. He was a sight to see.

I couldn't take my eyes off him. I sat there for a long time, watching as he worked his way through that pile of wood, splitting it so we'd have a fire over the winter. So he could keep us warm. And that brutal, fierce expression never left his face once.

He brought the ax down hard again, and I squirmed in my seat. Watching had made me hot and wet and aching. I always wanted him. Every night he had me, hard and unyielding. His body taking mine like he thought it was the last time. Rough-skinned hands moving my body where he wanted it. Deep, hungry kisses. I couldn't get enough of Cash's brand of loving.

He swung the ax once more, burying it in the large block he split the logs on, then he scooped up his shirt and started across the field. I turned back to my laptop and tried to focus, to get back into the scene I'd been writing, but the ache between my thighs was unrelenting.

The front door opening and closing reached me and had my heart racing faster. It did that a lot around Cash. Just knowing he was near. And I still hadn't gotten used to that gorgeous blue gaze. His eyes made my belly squirm every time he aimed them at me. God, all he had to do was look at me and I'd give him anything he wanted.

My breath quickened at the *thump* of his boots coming down the hall. The door opened and there he was, still shirtless, chest glistening, brow furrowed, beautiful blue eyes on me.

"You need something?"

I licked my lips. "You don't have to come all the way inside and ask me that. I can fend for myself. Though, thank you for the muffin and the tea. I probably would have forgotten to eat if you hadn't brought them to me. I was so caught up in writing, I didn't even notice."

His hands went to his hips. "I know."

His gaze didn't waver.

Having a husband who was a man of few words could be difficult at times. Like now. He was waiting for an answer, and I wasn't exactly sure what the question was. "Um...no, I don't need anything."

"You were watching me."

I flushed. Ridiculous with the things we'd done to each other, but still, getting caught perving at my new husband shirtless and chopping wood made me blush. Not much I could to about that.

I squirmed in my seat, and it squeaked again.

Cash's frown deepened, and he moved around the desk and crouched beside me, turning the seat with me in it to inspect it.

I shifted one leg to the side to give him room while he did this, as he moved his hand over smooth wood. And that just turned me on more.

"I'll fix it. Stop the noise."

"Thanks," I whispered, my voice husky from having him so close.

When his eyes lifted, they went right between my legs.

My massive husband stilled, then huffed out a breath before raising one of his hands, going right to the scrap of fabric covering me. He hooked his finger in it and yanked it aside.

I wasn't wearing any panties underneath, since I'd just pulled on the shorts after we'd had sex during the night. I flushed, imagining how swollen and wet and pink I probably looked from all my squirming while watching him work.

His nostrils flared and his gaze lifted to mine, eyes filled with heat. "How did this happen, wife?"

I shivered. I loved him like this. Craved it. "I was watching my husband chop wood with his shirt off. It's all your fault. I started to have all these...thoughts," I said shakily. "So really, it's your responsibility to make it better."

His gaze moved down my body, then back up, slowly, hungrily. "Yeah, it is," he said roughly.

He stayed on his knees but lifted from his crouch, hands going to the arms of the chair, boxing me in. "What thoughts?"

I trembled harder, so turned on now, so wet, it was almost embarrassing. "I...I..."

"Tell me," he rumbled.

Those blue eyes were locked on mine, looking deep, drawing me in until all I saw was Cash. "I imagined you coming in here like this...bending me over my lovely new desk and taking me from behind."

His big body shuddered. "Imagined doing the same thing while I made it."

"You did?" I asked, sounding as breathless as I felt.

He dipped his chin, then gripped my hips and jerked me forward so I was balanced on the edge of the seat. He hooked one long, thick finger around the fabric between my legs and pulled it aside again. "So wet."

My heart raced faster. "Yes."

"All for me?"

"Yes."

He dipped his head and breathed deeply, then growled like a ravenous beast. His hands gripped my butt, holding firm, and he moved in, dragging his tongue through the center of me.

I arched against his mouth, crying out—his tongue against my aching flesh was pure heaven. His fingers flexed against my butt cheeks, digging deep, holding me against his mouth. Holding me immobile. There was no wriggle room, no escape from him. He licked me, sucked me, played with me until I was fisting his hair and whimpering.

"I-I'm going to..."

His mouth was gone, right before I went over the peak. I cried out, an anguished sound. So achy and desperate for him to make me come. But I didn't have time to voice my protest because Cash lifted me out of the seat, spun be around, and bent me over the desk. My shorts were torn down my legs a moment later.

I felt him right behind me, yanking open his jeans.

His foot went between mine, forcing my legs wider, then the head of his cock was at my opening. He paused and ran his hands over my bare cheeks, and I arched, lifting my ass higher, desperate for him to take me.

He grunted his approval and thrust in. All the way. Filling me to the root.

I bucked against him and screamed out, my hands flying to the edge of the desk in front of me and gripping on tight as he dragged his cock almost all the way out and slammed back in. One hand was at my hip, the other sliding to the back of my neck, holding me down as he pounded into me over and over again.

"My wife wants to be fucked over her desk? That's what I'll give her."

I gasped and cried out. "Don't stop. Please, don't stop."

"Jesus, look at you," he said, and his voice broke. "So beautiful. The way you take my cock, Riley. Next time you need me like this, you come and get me."

"*Oh, please. Please. Please, Cash,*" I chanted, not knowing what I was begging for, just needing more, more of everything, more of Cash. Always more.

He bent over me, and one of his hands covered one of my own at the edge of the desk, the other sliding underneath, across my hips, and tugged me back from the edge of the desk.

His mouth went to my ear. "Can't get enough of my cock, can you, Riley?"

"No."

"You want it harder, don't you? Deeper?"

I sobbed. "Yes. Yes, I need it."

"I'll always give you what you need, wife. Always."

Then with a grunt, he gave me what I asked for, fucking me harder, deeper, and I sobbed again. This was amazing. What we had when we were together like this was better than anything I'd ever experienced. But I needed more. I needed Cash to let me see him. Really see him. I wanted what was in his heart.

And I wanted to make that heart mine.

I just wasn't sure he was capable of giving it to me. If he'd ever open up. If he'd ever let me in.

Then thinking was impossible as his hand slid lower, his fingers going between my thighs, working my clit.

My mouth dropped open, and Cash grabbed my chin, turning my head and taking my mouth in a brutal kiss as I came. I fed him my scream, and he groaned as he pulsed deep inside me, grinding, staying deep, prolonging it for both of us.

When I finally collapsed on the desk, Cash carefully slid from me, lifted me from my prone position, and swung me up into his arms.

I rested my head against his chest, too weak to wrap my arms around him. But it didn't matter; Cash had me. He carried me through the house and into the bathroom, and he kept me in his arms as he turned on the shower. While it warmed up, he stripped us both, then stepped inside.

He held me to him as he lathered me with soap, as he gently washed my hair. Every now and then he'd caress me. His hands sliding over my butt, cupping my breasts, between my legs, pressing kisses to my shoulders, the top of my head, my hand, wherever he could reach.

"You said your last hug...from your mom was ten years ago. Is that when you lost them, your parents?" I don't know why I asked, maybe because right then I was feeling so close to him and I wanted to try for that "more" I so desperately needed. He hadn't really talked about them at all since I'd moved here.

He stilled behind me.

"Cash?"

He cleared his throat.

"If it's too painful..."

"Yeah," he said abruptly.

Pain sliced through me. "That's awful. God, I'm sorry. Losing them in a car crash like that, while they were so far away in the city, must have been incredibly hard. But you never mentioned when it happened, and I...I want to know more. More about you. How long you'd been here without them." I tried to turn to face him, but he wouldn't let me.

"You know how they died?"

"Yes, you told me in one of your emails. When I asked you about your family." I tried to turn again—again he wouldn't let me, then his hands were gone.

The shower door opened and Cash climbed out.

Startled, I spun to face him. "Where are you going?"

"Got work to do."

He slung a towel around his hips and strode out of the bathroom, leaving me there alone. I stared at the shut door in shock. What just happened? Obviously, his parents and their death was hard for him to talk about, but rather than saying that, he'd walked away.

He'd shut me out. Again.

# 10

# CASH

RILEY MOANED as I thrust into her, my mouth on her breast, sucking on her nipple. I couldn't look away as she came for me in the darkness, as her beautiful, soft body arched up against me. Listened to my name on her lips as she came apart.

I let go then, coming hard inside her. Only then. When Riley was satisfied. I'd made her come over and over as an apology for walking out on her the day before in the bathroom.

I didn't like to talk about my parents or their accident. I never had talked about it. I'd felt blindsided when she brought it up. I assumed it would come up eventually, but I still hadn't been prepared for it.

But what had sent me running was her knowing how my parents had been taken from me, that I'd mentioned it in my emails. No, I hadn't done that. I'd told her they were gone but had never given details.

I pulled out of Riley and folded her in my arms. She was exhausted and drifted off moments later. I held her tighter. The book she'd given me when she first came here. The mention of chocolate cake. All things I'd apparently told her in my emails. It had confused me, but I'd been preoccupied with trying to make my wife happy, to not mess everything up. Now I couldn't get those things out of my head.

An unsettling feeling moved through me.

*Landon.*

He'd been our go-between since I didn't have a computer. He'd call, he'd read me Riley's emails, and I'd tell him what to reply with.

Anger pumped through me. Landon had added his own two cents. Had embellished my words. There was no other explanation.

RILEY WAS TAKING A BATH AND I WAS IN HER NEW OFFICE, snooping through her things. It felt wrong. It was wrong, but I wanted to see those emails. I opened her laptop and had to stop myself from throwing it across the room. I had no idea what I was doing. It was asking for a password. I rubbed my hands over my head in frustration.

Maybe she had it written somewhere. I yanked a drawer open, then another.

Several notebooks filled the drawer. I lifted them, and underneath was a stack of paper. I flicked through it.

Our emails. For some reason, she'd printed them.

I read through the first one and frowned.

Then the next, breathing harder, faster.

I scanned the rest, feeling sick.

He hadn't just added to them. He'd made me a completely different person. A man who had a lot to say. In these emails, he hadn't just said I liked to read. He'd given her book titles, favorite authors, my *feelings* about them.

There were drawn-out conversations on food, hobbies, politics, and the list went on. Landon had made me...interesting, cracking jokes, teasing her, sharing stories.

And then there was the stuff about my parents. It was all there.

When I'd called him and he'd read me her emails, he'd purposely left so much out, only giving me the parts that I'd expect.

*This* wasn't me. So much of this wasn't me.

Riley had come here expecting a completely different person.

A different man.

I stuffed the printouts back where I found them and strode through the door, right out of the house, rage pumping through me. I wasn't ready to talk to Landon, not yet. I needed to think, get my head around this. Why would he do this to me? He was one of my oldest friends. Had been friends with my parents.

*You know exactly why he did it.*

Because without his help, Riley would never have chosen me. She would never have wanted me.

She would never have come here.

What must she think? God, she must be so confused. Wondering what the hell was wrong with me. Why I was so different. I swallowed, my mouth dry, heart racing, palms sweaty. Was she disappointed I wasn't the man she thought, I was?

*Of course, she is.*

She thought she was marrying a man who had a lot to say. Who knew how to joke and tease. Who knew how to talk about his feelings.

She came expecting the opposite of me. Yes, I liked to read, but I didn't know how to have big philosophical conversations like Landon had with her about the books I'd read. I wasn't the deep-thinking man he'd made me out to be.

I hadn't even thought to ask any of the questions he had, not even when I got her here.

*Because you were just happy she came. That she wanted you.*

"Cash."

I turned. Riley stood at the door, a damp towel wrapped around her ample curves, skin pale and smooth. Her hair was wet and hanging around her narrow shoulders. I wanted to walk over to her, wrap her in my arms, and never let her go. Carry her to our bedroom and spend the rest of the day and night buried inside her.

Yesterday, I would have.

Yesterday, I didn't know the truth.

The man she thought she married was a lie. I was a lie. A fictional character, like in one of her books. Now what we had felt...dishonest. Even though I hadn't known what Landon had done, I did now. *Tell her. She deserves to know.*

I couldn't do it. I'd lose her, and I could not lose her.

"Don't stay out working too long," she called. "Dinner will be ready in an hour." She smiled at me, then went back inside.

I busied myself until it was time for dinner. Riley had made a chicken pie. One of my favorites. Something she'd learned about me from Landon. It was good, but I had to choke it down. My sweet, trusting wife was trying to give me everything I wanted, to make me happy. She was chatting away while we ate, trying so hard to make this work.

But now that I knew the truth, I became aware of the strain on her face. Could see the disappointment when I answered in my usual way. But I didn't know how to be anyone else. I didn't know how to be the man Landon created.

And when we went to bed later that night, for the first time in two weeks, we didn't...make love. That's what it had been for me, and I wanted her so bad it hurt not to take her, not to please her. But until I worked out what I was going to do, I couldn't bring myself to touch her, not like that.

"Cash?" she said into the darkness.

"Yep?"

"Are you okay?"

"Just tired," I muttered.

She snuggled into my side. "You've worked hard all day."

I didn't answer, swallowing convulsively as I wrapped my arms around her.

She was going to leave me.

As soon as she found out, she would leave. And I'd be alone again. But this time, I wouldn't survive it, not now that I knew how wonderful my life could be with Riley in it.

———

I WAS MAKING COFFEE WHEN THE SATELLITE PHONE RANG. I snatched it up in a bad mood. I was tired and confused, and I wanted to hold my wife. I wanted to make love to her, kiss her. Listen while she talked nonstop. She was in her office working, and I was out here avoiding her when what I really wanted was the complete opposite.

I put the phone to my ear. "Yeah?"

"Cash, it's Landon."

I clenched the phone tight and gritted my teeth. I was trying to work out what to say when he carried on talking.

"A cop from Denver called, spoke to Brady, wanted to

pass a message on to your Riley. He...ah...thought it would be better coming from me."

Brady was one of the local police officers. I gripped the phone tighter. "A cop?"

"She say anything to you about some guy named Keith?"

"No. She say anything to you?" I bit out.

There was a beat of silence. "Can't say that she did..." More silence. "You know, don't you?"

"Yep."

"Shit, I was just trying to help, boy. You've been on your own so long and I...your parents...wouldn't want that." He cursed under his breath. "Look, you can be pissed at me later. This is important."

"Then spit it out."

He cleared his throat. "Riley...she had a stalker back in Denver. This guy Keith is her ex-boyfriend. Anyway, he set about harassing and following her after they broke up. They couldn't prove it was him. Then he broke into her place one night, terrorized her for hours. He went into hiding. They finally found him, seeing as he's been going crazy looking for her since she moved out here, and he got careless. Cop wanted her to know they got the evidence they needed. He's been charged. And that it's...um...safe if she wanted to go home."

I stood rooted to the spot.

Home.

She *was* goddamn home.

"Cash?"

"Gotta go." I hung up and braced my hands on the counter, staring out the window.

She came to me to escape. She moved from her old life to get away from this creep stalking her.

*I know you'll keep me safe.*

She'd said that to me more than once. I'd assumed she meant while we were flying, but it was more than that, wasn't it?

Chances were good she hadn't been thinking clearly when she answered my ad. Fear will make a person do all sorts of things they usually wouldn't.

Maybe even marry a man they barely knew.

A man who didn't really exist.

And now the reason she'd come to me was gone.

There was nothing keeping her here anymore.

---

*RILEY*

The *thump* of Cash's boots grew louder.

I looked up from reading over the chapter I wrote yesterday to find him standing at the door. His expression was wary, his big frame held rigid.

Something was wrong. Nerves instantly fired to life in my belly. "What's going on?"

His jaw worked, and his gaze bored into me. The nerves got worse.

"What is it?" The words came out hushed. I took in the look on his face. I wasn't sure I wanted to know, anymore.

"Keith?"

I shot out of my chair. Was he here? Had Keith somehow found me? I tried to collect myself, my mind running in circles. "No. Does he know where I am...does he..."

"No. He's not here." Cash crossed his arms. "But a Denver cop wanted to pass on that they have the evidence they needed. That this *Keith* had been charged. He was stalking you?"

The muscles in Cash's arms bulged, the veins popping as he clenched and unclenched his massive fists.

*They'd caught him?*

Relief made my knees weak.

"Yes." I couldn't keep it from him anymore. At first, I'd been desperate to put it all behind me, and I'd continued to say nothing for the same reason. I hadn't wanted to bring Keith here, to my new life, even if it was just to talk about him.

"He was your boyfriend?"

My heart thundered harder, faster. "When I broke it off he...didn't want to let me go."

"He broke into your place and..." He thrust his fingers through his hair, his eyes flashing. "Terrorized you?"

I bit my lips to stop them quivering. Even though it was months ago now, I still woke at night sometimes with a scream trying to crawl up my throat, and sometimes there was no stopping it. "Yes," I whispered.

"What did he do?"

There was a growl to Cash's voice that lifted the hair on the back of my neck. "He just...he said some scary things, threatened me when I wouldn't tell him I...I loved him, when I wouldn't take him back. He...ah...had a knife and said he was going to cut me if I didn't do as he said. A neighbor heard me scream and called the police. He heard the sirens and took off. He's been missing since."

Cash stood like a statue, so still and silent it was unnerving.

"Cash?"

He spun suddenly and plowed his fist into the wall, punching a hole through it. I cried out in surprise, my hand flying to my chest. Then he stood there breathing heavily, body shaking hard.

"I'd never hurt you, Riley," he rasped.

"I know…"

"He hurt you. He scared you. He threatened you with a *knife*."

I hadn't known Cash long before I worked out he struggled with expressing his feelings. The way he had reacted just now wasn't great, but I knew this man well enough to know where it came from. I remembered what Birdie had said, that with men like Cash, a physical response came more naturally than a verbal one.

He cared about me. Maybe not the way I did him. But he took care of the things he considered his. I was one of those things now. He cared deeply for his family, would do anything for them, and now that family included me.

So I walked up behind him, and like I was approaching an injured animal, I slowly lifted my hands, resting them on his hips before carefully wrapping them around him.

I pressed my cheek to his back. "I'm okay, Cash. The police have him. It's over. And I have you now, to keep me safe, don't I?"

A shudder wracked his massive body as both of his hands covered mine, holding them, keeping my arms tight around him. We stood like that, no one saying anything, just me holding him and Cash keeping me there where he wanted me.

"The nightmares?" he rasped.

My eyes drifted closed. "Yes."

He took several more deep breaths, but he was still trembling with rage. Finally, he said, "I'll fix the wall." Then he lifted one of my hands, kissed my fingers, released me, and walked out.

I had no idea what he was thinking, what he was feeling. I went back to my chair and slumped into it.

How was I going to get through to him?

Would he ever let me?

---

CASH STAYED OUT LATE IN HIS WORKSHOP THAT NIGHT AND the next. And when he came to bed, I'd rolled into him, seeking his warmth and comfort. He'd held me, but there was a distance between us that had been impossible to miss.

He'd gotten up again this morning before I woke, and when he'd come in for lunch both days, he'd been subdued, closed off.

He was shutting me out. I could feel it.

It hurt deeper than any rejection I'd ever gotten from my parents.

I'd managed to finish my book the day before and sent it to my editor last night. Since I didn't have to write, I'd spent the day working on a surprise for him. I'd also made Cash a chocolate cake, and I planned to sit him down and make him talk to me, demand it, before things got any worse.

I missed him, and I didn't understand what I'd done wrong. Why he was withdrawing like this.

I turned to the door at the *thump* of his boots on the porch. Hunger usually drove him in around seven. He ate, but then he'd been going back out again. Not tonight. I was determined that we wouldn't go another night without sorting this out.

He walked in and stopped in his tracks, his gaze moving over me like it had the last two nights. Longing and wariness there, all rolled into one.

"Hope you're hungry? I made some of your favorites." I smiled, trying to get something back from him, anything.

"Steak and mashed potatoes and chocolate cake for dessert."

His jaw worked. "Thanks."

He strode to the kitchen and sat at his place at the table. I sat beside him, and we ate in silence for a few minutes.

"How is it?"

"Good."

He wouldn't look at me, and I couldn't stand it anymore. "Have I done something...to make you angry or upset?"

His fork froze on its way to his mouth, then his gorgeous blue gaze slid to me. For the first time, there was nothing. His stare was hollow. "No."

"It's just that you've been quiet and we're not...we haven't...had sex, and I don't know what I've done."

He put his fork down and sat back in his chair. "You haven't done anything, Riley. I'm busy, that's all."

My gaze dropped to his split knuckles from punching the wall. They'd scabbed over. I reached out and covered his hand with mine. "You can talk to me."

He stared down at my hand, throat working.

I grabbed what I'd made him from the chair beside me. "This is for you." I slid his plate out of the way and put the book down in front of him. "It's a scrapbook. It's filled with all the emails we sent each other. I don't think you know what they meant to me."

He stared down at it, body completely still.

I opened the cover, placing my hand over the first one. "Or how I felt when I saw that you'd replied. The happiness just reading your words gave me." I smiled at him. "Maybe one day we'll be able to show it to our children?" I squeezed his hand. "In your emails, you were..."

He stood suddenly, his chair sliding back hard, hitting the wall behind him.

I blinked up at him.

"Thank you for the...it's..." He swallowed convulsively. "I need to get back to work." He started toward the door.

"Cash..."

He paused by the door, shoved his fingers through his hair, and turned back to me. "I'm going away tomorrow, for a couple days. Hunting with Hank and Beau. You'll be okay?"

Would I be okay? As it was right now, I felt like I was all alone anyway. And I would not beg him to stay. I'd begged my parents to stay, and they'd left anyway. I wouldn't do that to myself again. Never again. "Yes," I whispered, glad when my voice didn't break.

He dipped his chin and walked out.

I cleaned up, showered, and went to bed. I woke when Cash climbed in beside me. He didn't reach for me. He stayed as far away from me as he could.

When I woke the next morning, he was gone. He'd left on his hunting trip.

And he hadn't even said goodbye.

## 11

## RILEY

As the plane came in to land, my heart was in my throat.

Three days Cash had been gone. Three days I'd been here on my own, wondering when he'd come back. Wondering what he was thinking. What he was feeling. If he even wanted me here anymore.

I felt like I didn't factor in his world, like I wasn't important.

I'd spent most of my life feeling that, and dammit, it hurt. So much.

He climbed out of his plane, looking extra rugged after three days of hunting, and despite it all—his silence, him not touching me, not saying goodbye when he left—I still had to stop myself from running to him, from throwing my arms around him.

Seeing him filled me with happiness and broke my heart all at the same time. I couldn't be with someone who was completely and utterly emotionally unavailable. Who would rather run away and hunt for three days than discuss what the real problem was.

All I could do was speculate. I'd been doing that since before he left.

And now I wasn't just hurt, I was angry as hell.

So when he walked in, did that jaw-clenching thing and dipped his chin in greeting, I lost it.

"Well, *hello* to you, too. Nice of you to finally come home." I planted my hands on my hips, fighting back tears when he said nothing. Refusing to let them fall. "Yes, I'm fine, thanks. Lovely of you to ask."

His wide chest rose, expanding on his deep breath. "Riley..."

I waited, but he said no more, his eyes boring into me, that square jaw working like he was trying to find actual words but none would come.

I threw my hands in the air. "You know what? Screw you." Then I spun and stormed to my office and slammed the door. Needing to get away before I fell apart in front of him.

Stupidly, I expected him to follow. He did not, and my anger reached new levels when the bang of the front door reached me. I spun to the window in time to see him walking across the field to his workshop. That was when I hit my limit.

That was when the pain I'd been fighting sliced through me so deep there was no way I could sit here and *wait* anymore.

I'd done that enough in my life.

Storming across the office, I yanked my door open, strode through the house, and marched outside. The barn door was closed, and I pulled it with such force that it swung back and hit the wall with a *bang* as I walked in.

Cash was standing at one of his workbenches, hands gripping the edge, head down. He swung around at my violent entrance. His massive body turning to face me, his arms dropping to his sides, his body going rigid.

I wanted him so bad I hurt.

All the anger and pain twisted together.

"Why are you being like this? Why won't you talk to me? Why is it that one moment you couldn't get enough of me and now you won't even look at me, let alone touch me? I need you to tell me, Cash. I need you to talk to me. I deserve that much."

He started breathing faster, heavier, but said nothing.

"Do you even want me here?"

Nothing.

The pain was like being cleaved in two. "I can't live like this," I whispered and stared into his eyes, needing to be reassured. Desperate for him to tell me he loved me, that he wanted me here with him. "I can't stay here…if things are like this."

He sucked in a sharp breath, his massive frame shaking, and made a sound like a wounded animal, but nothing else. Not one word.

"Goddamn you, Cash. Say something. Your wife just told you she's thinking of leaving." I walked up to him, the anger taking the lead, trying to protect my wounded heart, and I balled up my fist and thumped it against his chest. "Say something." Then I thumped both down on that wide chest and yelled at him, "Say something!"

He grabbed my wrists, but he didn't push me away, he held me where I was. He was shaking harder now, breath sawing in and out of him.

"Goddammit, Riley." He backed me against the wall, trapping me between him and the rough-sawn planks behind me.

"You left me. You made me feel like that sad little girl all over again, desperate to be loved but never good enough."

"Darlin'," he choked out.

A sob broke free. "What is wrong with me? Why does nobody want me?"

"No." He gripped my arms tight. "No, that's not...you were going to leave me sooner or later...and I thought... better for us both that it's now," he choked out.

I stared up at him stunned. "Why?" I whispered. "Why would I leave you?"

His eyes searched mine almost frantically. "Because I'm not the man you think I am. Because it was only a matter of time before you figured that out for yourself." He moved in closer, shaking harder. "Because every day you're here with me I need you more, want you more."

"Cash..."

"I didn't think I'd survive losing my parents, or the loneliness that came after. Then you came into my life, and the thought of losing you...it's worse, Riley. God, help me, it's worse."

My own breathing was ragged, and I wanted to touch him, comfort him, but he still held my wrists, stopping me from giving him what we both needed. "Please, Cash, I need you to tell me what's going on."

He leaned in closer, so much pain in his steady gaze. "When you gave me your scrapbook, the things you said...I knew then I had to give you up, that I couldn't lie to you anymore. You deserve more, more than me." His nostrils flared. "I didn't write those emails. I'm not him, the man you chose. That was Landon. I told him how to reply, but he took it upon himself to make them...*more*. He gave you more. Because he knew I wasn't enough. I wasn't enough to get you here, and I'm not enough to keep you, either."

I stared up at him in shock, not about the emails, I'd kind of begun to suspect that for myself, but that he would think that. That he could believe that about himself. "You're wrong."

His confused gaze searched mine. "Riley, I'm not..."

"I know *you*," I said. "I don't care who wrote those emails."

He shook his head, not listening. "I'm your husband, and you kept asking if I could keep you safe, and you were having *nightmares*. Christ, Riley, I missed it. Something was hurting you, scaring you, and I should have known. I failed you. I should have..."

"Cash..."

"Just tell me," he said, agony in his voice. "Did you come here to escape?" He leaned in, a ragged breath shaking from him. "Because...there's nothing keeping you here, not now that that asshole's been caught, now that you know the truth."

*What?* "Was Keith part of the reason I decided to search for something else, somewhere else? Yes, and I should never have kept that from you. But, Cash, as soon as I saw you...as soon as I looked into your eyes in that picture, I knew you were it for me. I just...knew. You think I don't know the real you? I've been living with the real Cash for nearly two months. *You*, Cash, are the quiet, stoic, hard-working, tender, generous, fiercely protective man standing in front of me. The man who showed me how much he loved his parents and cared for me by gifting me his mother's chair. The man who showed me how much he loves his cousins and their families by making the effort to see them regularly, who gets on the floor with the kids and plays with them and loves every moment of it."

He swallowed thickly. "Riley..."

"The man who cooks for me, who makes sure I'm warm by chopping wood for hours, or holding me safe and warm through the night. Who washes my hair when we shower. Who checks on me when we fly because you know I get scared, and who made me the office of my dreams just because you noticed I was sore after writing on the bed all day. The man who makes sure he's given me pleasure before he takes his own."

"Wife," he said, voice cracking.

I pulled my hands free, and he let me. I cupped his whiskered jaw. "Nothing's keeping me here? God, everything is keeping me here. *You* are everything, Cash Smith," I whispered, my lips trembling. "How could I miss it? You were showing me this whole time." I held his gaze. "You love me, don't you?"

"Yes," he said without hesitation. "So damn much. I'm sorry, sweetheart. I'm so sorry I hurt you."

I smiled wider. "And I love you, the man in front of me, not the man in those emails. *You*."

His arms came around me tight, that big body trembling as he buried his face between my neck and shoulder. "You love me? Promise you'll never leave me, darlin'. I don't want to be here, be anywhere without you."

I slid my hands up under his shirt, desperate to feel his hot skin under my hands, running them over his chest, then down his rigid abs. "You won't ever have to worry about that. I'm exactly where I want to be. With you. With my husband."

"I missed you so much." His hands roamed over me roughly, restlessly.

"I'm right here," I said as I popped open the button of his jeans and slid down the zipper. "I'll always be right here." I took his painfully hard cock in my hand, and he shuddered, his broken gasp tearing through me. "Let me show you how much I love you," I whispered and lowered to my knees in front of him.

His jeans sat low, his massive cock rock solid and weeping for my mouth.

"Please," he rasped.

That single word broke me. I'd give him anything. Do anything for this man. I certainly wouldn't make him wait. I gripped his heavy length and stroked him firmly as I leaned in and lapped at the glistening head. He bucked, a shout exploding from him. His hands shot out, and he planted them against the wall in front of him, like he needed to hold himself up.

I was trapped between the wall and Cash, his huge body looming over me. His head dipped, watching me as I sucked the head into my mouth and rubbed my tongue around the rim. Strain lined his ruggedly handsome face, and his blue eyes that I loved so much were fastened on mine.

He was letting me in, all the way, and I saw everything, right down to his beautiful soul.

I took more of him, stroking him with my hands, my mouth, taking as much as I could, desperate to make him feel good, to show him what he meant to me in a way he'd understand. Cash knew I loved him—I'd told him—but he was a man of action, not words. I wanted...needed to give him both.

---

CASH

I couldn't take my eyes off Riley on her knees in front of me, her heavy-lidded gaze holding mine captive. She owned me. Heart and soul. My sweet, fiery, little wife had stormed into my life and turned it on its head.

She sucked me deeper, and my knees nearly buckled under me.

I gripped the wall harder with one hand and reached down, cupping her precious face with the other. I clenched my ass and gritted my teeth, fighting the urge to thrust, but then she stroked me harder and swirled her tongue around the head. My control snapped.

I needed inside her.

Now.

I pulled from her mouth, gripped her arms, and tugged her to her feet. She was already shoving down her pants and underwear. She'd gotten them off one foot when I scooped her up, hooked her legs over my arms, pressed her into the wall, and thrust inside her.

She cried out, and I took her mouth, sliding my tongue deep. I needed to taste her, and she gave it right back to me. In this position, all she could do was take my relentless thrusts, just the way Riley loved it. I forced myself to slow down when all I wanted was to slam deep.

Instead, I dragged it out for both of us, nowhere near ready for this to end. I filled her slowly and slid back out, over and over, until we were both trembling. Riley was so wet, as hungry for me as I was for her. I rested my forehead against hers, our mouths brushing, shaky breaths mingling, and I fed off her little gasps and helpless moans as I moved inside her.

I'd been so scared of losing her that I'd pushed her away, trying to protect myself. Told myself it was for the best.

But nothing could protect me from the pain of losing her. I would never survive that.

Never.

She wasn't going anywhere, though. She was right here with me, and this was where she was staying.

"*Oh God*." Riley moaned.

"You need me to fuck you harder, wife?"

"*Yes*. Yes, I need it."

Her cheeks were pink, and her skin glistened. She was right on the edge—I could see it, feel it. I'd made us both wait long enough. I kissed her hard, deep, then lifted my head and watched her as I slammed in deep.

Riley's mouth dropped open, lips dark and swollen from my kisses, her eyes so heavy with lust I couldn't look away.

"Is this what my wife needs?" I asked as I thrust inside her.

"Yes. Always. I always need you…like this. Any way you give it to me," she cried. "I just need you. All of you."

"You have me," I growled as I thrust back in, deeper than before.

Riley screamed, and then she was coming, her pussy gripping and releasing me repeatedly. I couldn't hold back another minute, not while watching my woman in the throes of pleasure after not being close to her like this for so long, and not with the way she felt squeezing down on me.

I slid deep and roared, going over with her. We moved against each other until the last shudder, the last pulse of pleasure had worked its way through us.

When I was sure my legs were steady, I tugged up my jeans, shifted Riley in my arms, and, holding her tight to me, carried her inside, straight to our bedroom.

I laid her on the bed and finished undressing her, then I did the same. When I was lying beside her, I pulled her into my arms and held her tight. She held me back, just the same.

"Promise me you won't ever shut me out like that again," she whispered against my shoulder.

I pressed my lips to her hair. "I promise, darlin'." I kissed the top of her head. "I've been alone...I've been so lonely for so long, and I'm...I'm used to being in my own head. I'm not good at expressing myself. But I want to. I'll try harder from now on."

She lifted up, resting on my chest, and stared into my eyes, a small smile on her face. "I know." She kissed me softly. "But you're not alone anymore, Cash. I'll make sure you're never lonely again. We'll do that for each other."

I didn't have words for how hers made me feel, but this time it was okay. I knew it because Riley didn't give me a chance to answer. She kissed me again, and she didn't stop for a long time.

# EPILOGUE

CASH

LAUGHTER RANG out from the front porch.

I glanced over at the house and grinned. Riley was still giggling at something Freya had said as she headed inside. Birdie passed Freya the iced tea and laughed again. They always had a good time when they were together.

The house was full of family, of children, and Riley was in her element. Birdie had come armed with bags of baby clothes, and Freya had knitted a blanket.

Hank chuckled, and I glanced over. He was manning the barbecue while Landon chatted to him.

"You think you're ready?" Tucker asked, motioning to the herd of kids running by, shrieking and laughing, and handed me a beer.

"Yeah."

"He's ready," Hank said as he loaded the plate with meat and handed it to Beau.

"Who needs sleep anyway," Beau said, chuckling. "I haven't slept in years, and I'm doing awesome. The bags under my eyes have just made me more ruggedly handsome."

Tuck laughed, and Hank shook his head.

I glanced at the house again. Riley wasn't back outside yet, and lately having her out of my sight for any length of time made me uneasy.

I headed for the house. She'd had bad morning sickness at the start of her pregnancy, and she'd scared the hell out of me when she'd fainted, not once but three goddamn times. We only had a couple of months to go, but I was constantly worried about her. Terrified she'd faint again or fall.

I walked inside and worked my way through the house. The extension was finished, and right now all the rooms, including Riley's office, were being used for guests.

I found her where I should have looked in the first place. The nursery. She turned when I walked in, a soft smile on her beautiful face. I ate up the sight of her. She was wearing a cute little sundress that hugged her round belly, and her blond hair was down and wavy. She stole the breath right out of me.

She always did.

"Hey," she said.

"What you doing in here, darlin'?" I asked, pulling her into my arms.

"I came in to pee and ended up back in here when I was done." She rested her hands on my chest. "It's just so beautiful."

I'd finished it two days ago, and Riley loved it. This pleased me more than I was capable of expressing. "Glad you love it."

"More than love it." Her smile grew even wider. "How's the birthday boy feeling?"

Before Riley, I'd spent a lot of years not doing anything for my birthday. I'd been alone, and there hadn't been anything to celebrate. My Riley had gone through the same.

But she had insisted on having a party and used the fact that it would be her last chance to get together with everyone for a while as a way of bending me to her will. I would have said yes, anyway. I'd give her anything she wanted if it made her happy.

"What did Tucker bring you? Moonshine?"

"Yep." I tucked her hair behind her ear.

"Is he still having his...um...guest come to stay next month?"

Tuck was having a woman flown in, and I could tell Riley wasn't too happy about it.

"It seems wrong to me."

"Why?"

She frowned. "Why? Because he's paying her to...you know."

"He's not hurting anyone, darlin'. He's been using the same place for years and is careful about who he chooses. He has a good reputation there, and the women volunteer to come out here, which means he always has several to choose from. They make good money; he makes sure they have a good time. And honestly, I don't know what he does to them, but every woman I've ever flown out of there has ended up half in love with him."

Her eyes widened. "Really?"

I chuckled. "Yep."

"Why not do what we did? What Beau and Freya did?"

"Because he's not looking for a wife, just some company for a little while."

"Hmm."

I took her hand. "Come and eat."

"Okay, I could do with some cake."

It was late and I walked through the dark house. Everything was quiet.

A giggle came from the room most of the kids were bunking in down the hall. Someone else joined in. Then they were all cracking up. Yep, their parents could deal with that.

A grin curled my lips, and I headed to my and Riley's room. One day it would be our kids laughing and goofing around. I couldn't wait.

I walked in and Riley was tidying, picking up clothes. She was wearing one of my shirts, and it was huge on her. She'd started wearing them to bed when her pj's got too tight. I loved it.

"Leave that, darlin'. I'll pick it up."

She smiled softly at me. "I know you would. But I can do it. I'm fine, you know? I'm not going to faint again."

I moved up behind her and wrapped my arms around her, my hands on her belly. "You don't know that."

"I feel good. Full of energy, if you want the truth."

I took the shirt she was folding from her hands and led her to the bed. "That's great, darlin', but right now, you're gonna rest."

"So bossy." She narrowed her eyes at me. "When did that happen?"

I shrugged, smirking down at her.

She shook her head. "Bossy," she muttered again but did as I asked.

I switched off the light, undressed, and climbed into bed. Riley rolled against me like she always did.

"Cash?"

"Hmm?"

"I can't sleep."

"You've been trying for barely a minute." I grinned into

the darkness. I knew what that breathy note to her voice meant. We had a lot of sex, but since she'd become pregnant she was insatiable. Her hormones were out of control, and I sure as hell wasn't complaining.

She pressed her face to my chest and curled her knee over my thigh, her hand gliding across my stomach. "Stop toying with me. You know what I want."

She tipped her head up for a kiss, and I gave it to her.

"Climb on, then, darlin'," I said against her lips.

Her breathing grew heavier, quicker as she did as I said. She tore the shirt off over her head and straddled me. I glided my fingers between her thighs and groaned.

"So hot, sweetheart...drenched," I rasped.

She dragged her hands down my chest. "I've been thinking about this all day. We missed our midday snuggle."

I chuckled. Snuggling was involved but not until after I'd made my wife come several times.

She lightly hit my shoulder and giggled. "Smart-ass."

"I didn't say anything. Now are we gonna get on with snuggling or are you just gonna sit there naked and drive me crazy?"

She gripped my hard cock and lifted up, positioning me. I held her hips, steadying her, and bit back my growl when she sank down, taking all of me. Riley moaned and, planting her hands on my chest, rolled and rocked her hips, keeping me deep as she did.

Her hair fell forward, and I brushed it back, needing her eyes on me. I cupped her cheek. Christ, she was lovely moving on top of me, bathed in moonlight.

"You take my breath away," I said, something I would have only thought a year ago, something I would have struggled to share.

Her hand covered mine, and she sucked my thumb into

her mouth. My hips jerked and my balls grew tight. I pulled it free before she made me come too fast, and she held my gaze, making my heart beat faster.

I brushed her clit with my wet thumb, and it didn't take long before she grabbed my hand and lifted it to cover her mouth, getting me to muffle her cries. Seeing her like that, feeling her gripping me, I came with her.

When she finally went limp, I caught her up in my arms and laid her beside me, pulling her in close again.

"Love you, Cash," she said sleepily. "Thanks for the snuggle."

I grinned up at the ceiling, chuckling under my breath. "Love you, too, wife. And you know I'm here for the snuggles any-damn-time."

# ABOUT THE AUTHOR

Sherilee Gray is a kiwi girl and lives in beautiful New Zealand with her husband and their two children. When she isn't writing sexy, edgy contemporary and paranormal romance, searching for her next alpha hero on Pinterest, or fuelling her voracious book addiction, she can be found dreaming of far off places with a mug of tea in one hand and a bar of Cadburys Rocky Road chocolate in the other.

**To find out about new releases, sales, giveaways and other cool stuff, sign up for my newsletter!**

## ALSO BY SHERILEE GRAY

**The Smith Brothers:**

*Mountain Man*

*Wild Man*

*Solitary Man*

**Rocktown Ink:**

*Beg For You*

*Sin For You*

*Meant For you*

*Bad For You*

**Knights of Hell:**

*Knight's Redemption*

*Knight's Salvation*

*Demon's Temptation*

*Knight's Dominion*

**Lawless Kings:**

*Shattered King*

*Broken Rebel*

*Beautiful Killer*

*Ruthless Protector*

*Glorious Sinner*

*Merciless King*

**Boosted Hearts:**

*Swerve*

*Spin*

*Slide*

*Spark*

**Axle Alley Vipers:**

*Crashed*

*Revved*

*Wrecked*

**Black Hills Pack:**

*Lone Wolf's Captive*

*A Wolf's Deception*

**Stand Alone Novels:**

*Breaking Him*

Printed in Great Britain
by Amazon

11497388R00082